A FATHER'S INSISTENCE

DARK SOVEREIGNTY BOOK THREE

ANNA EDWARDS

Vichy
Learn to swim
Chris
Chiara

CONTENTS

Foreword	vii
Chapter 1	1
Chapter 2	11
Chapter 3	21
Chapter 4	29
Chapter 5	37
Chapter 6	45
Chapter 7	53
Chapter 8	61
Chapter 9	69
Chapter 10	79
Chapter 11	87
Chapter 12	95
Chapter 13	101
Chapter 14	109
Chapter 15	117
Chapter 16	125
Chapter 17	133
Chapter 18	143
Chapter 19	151
Chapter 20	159
Chapter 21	169
Chapter 22	177
Chapter 23	185
Epilogue	197

Acknowledgments	203
The Control Series	205
The Glacial Blood	207
Because He's Perfect Anthology	209
About the Author	213
Meet the Author	215

Copyright © 2019 by Anna Edwards

All rights reserved. No part of this publication may be reproduced, distributed or transmitted in any form or by any means, without prior written permission.

www.AuthorAnnaEdwards.com

This is a work of fiction. Names, characters, places, and incidents are a product of the author's imagination. Locales and public names are sometimes used for atmospheric purposes. Any resemblance to actual people, living or dead, or to businesses, companies, events, institutions, or locales is completely coincidental.

Warning: This book contains sexually explicit scenes and adult language and may be considered offensive to some readers. This book is for sale to adults only, as defined by the laws of the country in which you made your purchase.

Disclaimer: Please do not try any sexual practice without the guidance of an experienced practitioner. Neither the publisher nor the author will be responsible for any loss, harm, injury, or death resulting from the use of the information contained in this book.

Cover Design by www.CharityHendry.com

Logo Design by Charity Hendry

Editing by Tracy Roelle

Formatting by Charity Hendry

Proofreading by Sheena Taylor

A Father's Insistence/ Anna Edwards -- 1st ed.

ISBN 978-1795553513

❀ Created with Vellum

FOREWORD

Please note this is a dark romance. There will be triggers including rape and murder.

Thank you for understanding. I hope you enjoy reading.

Anna xx

CHAPTER ONE

THEODORE

"She looks just like you." I bring my newborn niece up into my arms and gently rock her while she coos quietly. "Thank you for allowing me to come and see her." Looking out of the corner of my eye, I can see Nicholas and William standing sentinel: one at the door to the lounge, and the other by the patio doors to the garden. These are the only exits to the newly rebuilt and decorated room I am currently sitting in, and they are being covered in case I should decide to make a run for it with baby Rose. Tamara sits opposite in a smart suit with her hand resting over the small swell to her stomach. I guess she's here in case of any potential litigation.

Judging by the size of her, she can only be a few months pregnant, but when we entered the room, William was already playing the protective soon-to-be father. I'm not here to cause trouble, though. I just want to check on my sister and my niece, but that doesn't stop me from looking down my nose at Nicholas Cavendish for being my niece's father. He's not the man I would have chosen for my sister.

"I don't know," Victoria muses and strokes her daughter's head. "I think there's a lot of Nicholas in her. I've seen a couple of pictures of him when he was a baby, and they look so similar. You'll have to bring over a picture of me next time."

"You could come to our house?"

Victoria looks over to Nicholas, and I see him shake his head.

"I'm sorry. It's better that you come here."

The fury I carry around with me starts to burn a fire in my veins. Nicholas Cavendish is obviously controlling my sister. I want to see her free and happy away from him without the act she's putting on in front of me. It sickens me he's abusing his position of power to do god knows what to my sister. My father told me about the society and why he feels the need to change it. He told me of how the previous Duke was trying to steer it away from the abuses that were being inflicted upon women, but Nicholas and William killed their father, so they could take over. He told me he'd had no choice but to give my sister to Nicholas, because Nicholas would have ruined us all and taken Victoria and killed her, otherwise. I don't want to believe it's true, and I have to be honest with myself and say that Victoria seems happy, but I saw the sadness behind my father's eyes. He was a broken man the day he told me everything. He'd given his daughter away to a life of torture—it was enough to destroy any father. Something inside me snaps at

Nicholas' refusal to allow Victoria to visit her childhood home, and before I can think about what I'm saying, my mouth opens in an uncontrollable outburst.

"And why can't she visit her childhood home? Are you scared that by being out of your presence for a few minutes she might actually see sense and report you to the police for your crimes against women?"

The room goes silent. Even little Rose seems to sense the tension and stops her cute baby noises. Nicholas breaks the impasse by pushing his tongue against his teeth and inhaling. The resulting hissing noise echoes in the large room.

"Theo please?" Victoria pleads and tries to take her daughter back from me.

"I should walk out of here now with Rose before you have a chance to sell her to the highest bidder."

Nicholas still doesn't say anything, but the edges of his face are flaming red, and I know he's trying to control his temper. William, who's standing by the door, swipes at his ear and then his head. His mouth is moving, and if I'm not mistaken, I'm sure he's reciting mathematical equations. I'll never understand these two brothers. They are both insane.

I want to test Nicholas' limits. Maybe I can walk out of here with my sister and her daughter? Pushing to my feet from where I've been sitting, I cradle Rose tighter to my chest, and she whimpers a little.

"Th-Theo..." Victoria stammers quietly.

"William, Tamara," Nicholas finally speaks. "I thought you had a doctor's appointment at twelve thirty. You don't want to be late. Hearing the heartbeat of your baby for the first time is a wonderful experience."

William pushes away from where he was casually lounging against the frame of the patio doors, and going over to Tamara, he assists her to her feet. Nobody says anything. I hold Rose tightly, waiting and watching to see what will happen next.

"It was good to see you again, Theodore." William bows his head at me and leads Tamara out of the room. She looks over her shoulder and takes a last sorrowful look toward me before leaving with her husband. We've never addressed the vicious lies she spouted at me the last time we met when she told me she was my half-sister, and that my father had raped her mother. It's something I can never forgive her for, but I don't doubt it's the Cavendish brother's influence that instigated them.

Nicholas strides over to Victoria and kisses her on the cheek.

"I need to make a phone-call to Prince John. I'll leave you and your brother to talk. You don't need me here." She reaches up to him with her hand, which he takes and gently squeezes before placing a kiss on it and letting go. He comes closer to me, and my hands involuntarily tighten on Rose. His eyes are focused squarely on his daughter, and I know he's going to take her with him, but he surprises me when he bends down and kisses her on the head.

"Enjoy you time with your uncle, my little button. Daddy will be back later." Rose replies to him with baby babble as if she understands him, which she doesn't, of course, since she's only a few weeks old and probably can't even see him properly yet. Then Nicholas turns his attention back to me.

"I'm sorry your views of me are tainted. I can assure you I have nothing but respect and love for my wife and daughter although I know you don't believe it. I need to protect my family, however. It's the only reason I won't allow them to visit you at your home. You're always welcome here though. Victoria will always be your sister and Rose your niece. My brother and I will not stop you from seeing them. I shouldn't have been here today…it was wrong, and I'm sorry. Please, stay as long as you want." Nicholas then bows his head to me, which is something he doesn't have to do since he's a Duke, and I'm only the son of a Viscount. I have no title, yet, and should defer to him. I can't though. Despite his words, I know this is all merely a part of whatever game it is he's playing, so I don't show him the same respect back. He sighs heavily and leaves the room.

"Why do you have to be this way?" Victoria immediately chastises me. "Why can't you accept he's a good man?"

"Because I know differently," I reply and hand Rose back to her when my niece starts to fuss.

"You only know what our father has told you."

"Then you tell me the truth. Tell me what is really happening here," I demand as Victoria settles Rose against her breast to feed her while stroking her daughter's head underneath a strategically placed blanket.

"Are you even willing to listen to the truth?" Victoria questions.

"I just want to know you're safe, and while you're here, I don't think that is the case." I let out a long-frustrated sigh. "Tell me honestly, sister, two things: Do you have the society's crest burned into your thigh? And has Nicholas led you around naked in front of other members of the society?"

"That's what he told you?" Victoria's eyes fill with unshed tears.

"Our father? Yes, he told me how you were paraded like a dog and had your skin permanently branded. Did Nicholas do that? Did he hurt you in that way?"

"Yes…but…" she begins to protest to me. No doubt, she wants to tell me about how he's a good man, now, but her words will fall on deaf ears. Any man who could do that to the woman he's supposed to love will always be the devil to me, and my sister knows it. She stops all conversation and focuses on her daughter. There is little point in me staying here since it's obvious I can't save my sister today, and the guilt of that starts to twist in my stomach.

"If you ever need me, just call. You'll always be my sister, no matter what."

I leave Victoria in the room, and as I shut the door, I can hear her softly sobbing. Nicholas is standing in the hallway and on the phone as he told me he would be.

"I'll call you back in a minute, John." He hangs up. I'm done, though. I can't be in this place anymore. The burden of the suffering, which has taken place within these four walls, weighs heavily on me. Without saying another word, I turn heel and stride straight out the front door leaving it open behind me.

It's not until I'm home and getting ready for bed, later the same evening, that I feel remotely calm after the meeting. I want to be a part of my sister's and my niece's life, but while they're under the thumb of Nicholas Cavendish, I've got no hope—I can't have while imagining the cruel way he's treating them. I might never get Victoria away from him. She's too far under the evil Duke's spell, but I have to save Rose. I can't let her be raised in a household where her father treats women as sex slaves.

I wish my father was here. I've had some cryptic messages from him over the last few months, but I've not physically seen him since the day he went into hiding because he was going to be questioned for Elsie Bennett's murder. He didn't kill her. My father is a good man. Okay, my mother and him had an interesting relationship—they weren't overly affectionate, and

I think that's why they live separately now. I barely see my mother. But that doesn't make him the man Victoria and Tamara claim him to be. He gave Elsie a home when she became a single mother with no family who could support her, and she'd nowhere else to go. He even paid for Tamara's education at Cambridge. If it wasn't for him, she wouldn't be a lawyer, now. Not that she seems to be rushing to go into practice. No, she's exploiting everything he helped pay for by using it against him in her position as the Cavendish brother's legal adviser. It's ungrateful and disloyal. He's never hurt Tamara, only helped her. Even more upsetting is the fact my father was always a loving and doting parent to Victoria. I remember them playing happily together in the gardens. I know he was strict with her and prevented her from going to university, which was sometimes a bone of contention between them, but it's not a reason for her to turn against him as she has. I guess she blames him for what she had to endure at Nicholas' hands.

"Ugh!" I exclaim and lash out at the wall closest to me. "Everything is a big mess."

I've drank half a bottle of brandy to try and ease my worries since returning from Oakfield Hall. I'm tired, frustrated, and just need to shower and sleep. Decision made, I undress and drop all my clothes in a pile on the floor. I've my own personal butler now my father's gone, and I know even though I should pick everything up he won't mind doing it for me when I'm so exhausted.

My father told me I could move into his rooms during his absence, but I've chosen to stay in mine, preferring them to the grandeur of his decoration. I've always been more of a simple man. After school, I went to Oxford University and studied business. I really enjoyed my time there and made many friends who I'm certain will be associates for life, but I've always known I'm destined for the title of Viscount, so I've not tried to branch out on my own. My father has drilled it into me since birth that I'm his heir, and he wants me ready to take over his title when I'm called upon to do so, eventually. I wouldn't be in a position to do that if I was knee-deep in running my own business. It's a little sad, because I had a fabulous idea for a company: assisting children with learning difficulties to get better exposure to the art of the world. Victoria had always been in love with art of any kind, and I'd seen first-hand on a work experience trip at university how it inspires children. Sadly, my future wasn't to travel down that path, though...maybe one day? Until then, I'm running the estate in my father's absence.

I step in the steaming shower and allow it to wash my worries away. I'm full of tension. Moving my hand down to my dick, I give it a few strokes to bring it to life. It's the easiest way to relieve my mood. It's completely at odds with the worries I have for my sister, but damn, I'm a man, and the way to my heart is through my dick. It's the only way to ensure I get some sleep tonight. I had a girlfriend for a short while at university, and I bring to mind the memory of her bouncing on my dick with her perfect tits rising and falling as she rode me like a cowgirl. My hand strokes faster and faster until my boys tighten, and my cum shoots off like a bullet into the shower wall. I feel all the tension ease from my taut body, and I yawn. Turning the water off, I reach for a towel and dry myself. I clean my teeth and do a final piss for the night before heading into my bedroom. Sliding between the luxurious sheets of my massive bed, my eyes instantly shut, and presumably I fall asleep because it feels like hours later when I'm awoken by a crash in the room.

"Theodore, it's just me," my father announces, and I rub my eyes still full of sleep.

"Father?"

He holds his finger to his lips while another man with him points a torch in my direction. Movement to my left captures my attention, and I look up just in time to see another man press a needle into my neck.

"What the fuck?" I exclaim. The world starts to spin as my head fogs with exhaustion again. "What's going on?" I slur, fighting to keep my eyes open.

"It's ok. It's the quickest way," my father reassures me, and before I can question him further...the world turns black.

CHAPTER TWO

JOANNA

The last few days have probably been the most peaceful of the year I've spent in captivity. I've not seen anyone apart from Camilla when she's dropped my food off. Today's meal was a bit more elaborate than the others. Most of the time, it's been a standard fair of brown toast for breakfast followed by a sandwich of some sort for lunch, and then fish or chicken with vegetables and potatoes for dinner. I've lost so much weight the clothes I was originally given now hang off my skeletal frame. I wasn't a big person a year ago, but I wasn't a skinny supermodel size either. I liked my food, especially steak, and I had a terrible weakness for chocolate. My favorite dessert was one of those chocolate cakes where the middle was still like molten lava. My mouth waters at the thought of it while my stomach cramps at the richness of the steak I've just eaten. Why after so long would they give me a steak? I can't help but think of myself as a prisoner on death row, and the meal I've just eaten is my last. If it is, I'm ready. I've got nothing left to live for. I don't know what living is anymore. I'm a girl whose father gave her away only to be sold to a monster. I've thought often about the other girls from that terrible night and wonder what has happened to them. I know the man who bought me is the father of one of them. I guess he exchanged one woman for another in effect. He told me once that she'd married Nicholas Cavendish. I can't help feeling sorry for her, wondering whether she or any of the other girls are still alive. No, if I'm to die tonight, I'll welcome it. I've been trained to within an inch of my life to obey Viscount Hamilton's rule, and should I fail, I'm fully aware of the disastrous consequences. I don't want to be raped by him anymore. I just want to go to sleep and never wake up.

I push aside the book I've been engrossed in for the last hour—reading provides the only form of sanity I've not been deprived of, yet—and getting to my feet, I stretch my legs and arms. The steak was far too rich for me, and my stomach still doesn't feel right. I'm rubbing it to relieve the discomfort when I hear my door being unlocked, and Camilla comes barging in. Without saying a word, she grabs me by the wrist and drags me from the room.

"No!" I try to force my feet into the ground, but she's too strong.

"Shut up," she shouts at me and whips her hand across my face. I reel back in shock. Although I'm used to beatings, I wasn't expecting that tonight. Camilla is joined by a man who lifts me off my feet and carries me down the hall. I initially panic before a calm sense of fate descends over me. This must be it...the moment I die. Why do I feel so happy? I surely shouldn't. After death, there is nothing: no coming back, no feelings, no pain. The. End.

I'm deposited into a room where the Viscount is already standing. It figures he would want to be the one to finish this. I kneel down before him as I've been taught.

"I warned you the time was approaching for you to fulfill your destiny, didn't I?" He informs me, patting the top of my head.

"Yes," I reply quietly. A speck of dust catches my eye on the floor, and as I let out a breath, the dust flutters along like an angel on a floating cloud. I wonder if I'll get wings? I must have earned them. Death can't be *it*...all there is left when life in this world ends. I've always believed in some sort of afterlife. Men like Viscount Hamilton deserve it, so they can be punished for their atrocities in this life. They can't just end. I have to know that somewhere they'll suffer for what they've done. My breath catches at the thought of there being nothing. This being the end for me. My twenty-two years on this planet equating to little more than an abuse victim who dies at the hands of her tormentor. I'm too busy trying to remember how to breathe when the first punch comes. Any chance I had of getting air into my lungs is ruined when pain explodes into them, instead. Several more hits rain down on me, and I curl into a little ball, desperately trying to protect myself. It doesn't work, though, and I know I'll be bruised tomorrow...if I'm still alive. I'm pulled to my feet by my frizzy, blond hair. My father always hated my hair with its natural curl. He said it left me looking like a wild child who'd been dragged through a hedge backward—an image I most definitely resemble, currently.

"You remember what you've been taught. I'm going to have to trust you from this point on, but remember I'll always be watching. I'll be there should you falter, ready to bring down hell upon you if you ruin this. I'm your master, your ruler, your everything. Without me, you'd be dead," Viscount Hamilton spits into my face. "Get her dressed," he orders, and my clothes are ripped from my body. Red marks, precursors to bruising, litter my porcelain skin. I'm forced into a white linen dress like the one I wore the night I was given to Nicholas Cavendish. I've traveled full circle. I'm back there, waiting to discover what my future will be, and only too aware of the trials. I'd been taught about them as I'd grown up, but my part in the Oakfield Society was short-lived. I was not one of the chosen girls, and I was sold off instead. I sometimes think the trials would have been easier than this existence.

Camilla grabs my hair out of the hands of the man who's been holding it tightly and rips a brush through the dry and tangled ends. I have my own shower, so I am able to keep clean, but the products aren't really suitable for my type of hair. I need a good haircut and conditioning treatment. I suppose, if I'm to die, it doesn't really matter. From the little I know of God, I don't think he's the type of person to judge someone for the style of their hair as they enter through the pearly gates.

Viscount Hamilton looks down at his phone when it makes a sound.

"He'll be here soon."

Camilla finishes re-arranging my hair and pushes me back down to my knees in front of Viscount Hamilton. The man who's terrorized every moment of my last year, both awake and asleep, pulls my chin up, so he can bore his penetrating gaze directly into me. I want to shut my eyes, but I know I can't, and even if I did, I couldn't block him out, because he's burned into my senses: I can see the little curl of his lip when he's enjoying what he does to me, I can hear the grunts of his exertions, and I can smell the foul stench of his breath as he kisses me all over my face. The steak sitting in my stomach bubbles, and I can't stop myself from heaving and then vomiting on the floor.

"What the fuck?" Viscount Hamilton steps back to avoid getting any on his designer leather shoes. "I was being nice to you and have provided you with a good meal, and this is what happens. You better not mess up your task, Joanna. You've been prepared. You've been trained, and you *will* lead us to untold power."

My head is spinning from the sickness and the beating. I've no idea what he's talking about.

"My son is nearly here. He'll be your husband within the hour, and you will take him straight to your room and make a child. You've been left in peace the last few days because your contraceptive injection ran out. He'll take you tonight, and together you'll make a boy capable of ruling over the Oakfield Society. One who will run it properly, not like the Cavendish brothers."

A bell sounds somewhere in the house.

"Get her up." I'm dragged to my feet, and a blanket is wrapped around me. Camilla brings me into her arms and buries my head into her chest. It's almost as if she's comforting me, but I know the things this woman is capable of, and it's nothing of the sort: it's an act. Everything happening here is designed for a purpose. The beating, the outfit, the fake show of sympathy are all part of a show. The game continues, and I'm still a pawn in it. I'm not going to die today, but something much worse is about to happen: I'm about to be married to a man who doesn't have a clue about the world he lives in.

I shift my head just in time to see two men enter the room, dragging a comatose body between them. A priest follows behind with his long garments flowing along the floor, and a bible in his hand. I would expect him to look shocked at the situation he's seeing, but he looks all too accepting and comfortable. He's clearly been hired specifically for his ability to turn a blind eye to the half-asleep groom and the battered bride.

"Theo," Viscount Hamilton addresses his son. I recognize him vaguely from society functions we both attended growing up. He was always one of the confident men in the background, surrounded by women but not particularly interested in anyone. It appeared to me his behavior was guided by his responsibilities to his family name. He was never one to use his future title to advance himself, though. Not like Nicholas Cavendish who used his on more than one occasion to get a girl into bed.

The men lower Theo into a wing-backed chair, and I can see he's trying his hardest to open his eyes.

"Father?" he groans and rubs his face. "What's going on?"

The Viscount brushes his hand against his son's shoulder, pretending to be the kind and caring father.

"I'm sorry for the subterfuge, my boy, but it's all necessary. I'll explain later. First, we need to make sure that this woman is safe, and there's only one way to do that. You need to marry her."

"Marry her?" Theo looks up confused. His eyes keep opening and closing. He's struggling to come out of whatever drug-addled state they've put him in. "I don't understand."

"I couldn't save your sister, Theo, please. We have to save Joanna."

I'm thrust forward nearer to the father and son who are

currently engaged in a conversation, which will shape my future.

"Joanna?" Theo rubs his head again. "Can I get water?"

The Viscount nods at one of the other men in the room. Minutes ago, they were beating me, but now they look as though butter wouldn't melt in their mouths. They are devils in disguise. A glass of water is brought over to Theo, and he drinks it down before trying to focus more fully on me, standing before him. I look down at my hands, and I realize they are shaking. I try to control them, but my body acts like it's not attached to my brain.

"Theo, this is Joanna. My men have just rescued her. She's been held captive by the Cavendish brothers for over a year now."

I raise my eyes from the son to the father. Shock should probably register on my face, but my body is numb to anything by this point. This is the plan, and I must follow it.

"Is that true?" Theo asks, his words still slurred, and his eyes still closing every now and then as he fights to stay alert.

"Yes, sir," I reply like a programmed robot. Viscount Hamilton smiles at me from behind his son's back.

"We don't have much time, Theo. The Cavendish brothers will be searching for us. I need to send them a message."

"Can I just get my head straight? Why did you have to drug me?"

"I didn't want to. I didn't have time to explain. I had to get back here."

Theo pushes gingerly to his feet and sways. He keeps one hand on the chair but reaches out with the other to me.

"Do you understand what's happening?" he asks as his hand rests on my shoulder. I can feel weight behind it and know he's using me, as well as the chair, for support.

I flick my stare quickly to the Viscount, and his eyes darken with the promise of a fury so great it will eclipse anything that has occurred before should I not give the correct answer.

"I don't fully understand anything at the moment. All I know is I don't want to go back into that room. I don't want to be tortured the way I was. I want help, and if what everyone is telling me will give me that, then I'll do it." My voice breaks with the honesty of my words and the lies mixed in. A lone tear trickles from the corner of my eye and tumbles down my cheek, following a path of guilt and utter bewilderment at the situation.

"Do it," Theo instructs the priest without any further thought. He lets go of the chair, and testing how close I'll let him come to me, he brings me into his arms. We support each other as the priest carries out the ceremony to make us man and wife. Theo signs the marriage documentation with effortless ease, but my hands shake so much my signature is barely legible.

"You're safe, now," Theo reassures me. He is becoming more alert as time passes. I want to scream at him that he's being played for a fool by his father, but I know I can't. It's too late to stop what is already in process.

The priest proclaims us man and wife, and the ceremony ends with subdued cheers from the gathered witnesses. It's not how I pictured my wedding when I was younger. There's no rejoicing crowds, beautiful bouquets, or a luxurious white silk dress. I don't love my husband, and I'm terrified of what comes next. Mind you, that's probably the same for any virgin bride, not that I'm a virgin anymore. I was when this all started, but that changed the day I was bought.

"You should take your wife up to your room to rest," Viscount Hamilton advises my new husband.

"What?" Theo blinks at his father.

"I'm not sure when she last slept properly."

"Of course."

"We'll talk more tomorrow. It's been a long day for all of us."

I look at the grandfather clock standing in a corner of the room when it starts to chime, and I notice it's just gone past midnight. Three hundred and sixty-six days in captivity, and yesterday wasn't my last day on this Earth.

Theo takes my hand and stumbles in a dream-like state from the room with me following, and Camilla leading the way. I turn my head back to take one last look at the Viscount before the door closes. He purses his lips together and mouths one word that sends shivers down my spine.

"Baby."

CHAPTER THREE

THEODORE

I'm not entirely certain whether I'm awake or still in a dreamlike state after being injected with that drug. This should be a dream because otherwise, fuck, I just married a stranger. However, the ice-like hand of the tiny woman who's following me into the grand bedroom of a house I've never seen before is all too real. I'm married. Shit! I don't understand any of this, but the instant I saw Joanna's hands shaking with fear, I knew I had to protect her. She's little more than a bag of bones with fading bruises that shadow her eyes, and I'm sure under the white linen dress she's wearing there'll be more. She's broken. I only need to see the distance in her eyes to know that. What she must have suffered is beyond comprehension to me. There is a part of me that wants to run from the room, find Nicholas Cavendish, and murder him with my bare hands. But the sane part, which is probably still a little worse for wear from the drugs, knows I can't do that. I have to stay here. I have to protect her. I have to give her life again...if that's even possible.

I let go of her hand, and she goes over to the bed. It's king-sized, covered in freshly laundered sheets. She looks at me and then at the bed. I watch her, still unsure of what is real and what is a dream. Slowly, she lifts the linen dress over her head and underneath, she's naked. I can see old and new bruising to her body. Scars from wounds mark her perfect skin, and I fight hard to tamper down the rage surging through me. She drops to her knees and bows her head.

"How would you like me, sir?" she offers in a voice so delicate it snaps my resolve.

"I don't!" I tell her and stomp forward. I grab her arm, and she whimpers. My head is screaming at me to calm down and be level-headed around her, but my heart is filled with fury, overruling any sensible thought. This girl has been through so much and has just offered herself to me.

"I'm your wife. We must do..." She tries her hardest to express what should happen next, but she can't. The words seem to stick in her throat—the mention of what normally comes after a wedding, silencing her. I throw her onto the bed, and as she parts her legs, ready for me, I turn away.

"Put the covers over you."

"*Please*," she pleads, and I can't hear any movement of her doing as I ordered.

"Joanna, cover yourself up." I swallow deeply. "Now!" The word leaves my mouth as an authoritative order, and I instantly hear her scrambling to do as instructed. I turn back to find her sitting in the bed with the sheets pulled up to her neck. "Thank you...stay here and get some sleep. Nobody except me will be allowed in here. I'll be back later."

"Where are you going?" She shifts to try and get out of the bed, but I put my hand up to halt her.

"Stay."

"I have to..."

She starts, but I cut her off.

"You don't have to do anything but sleep. Get some rest." I find myself at her side. I stroke my hand down her cheek, and she lets me without showing any fear of the possible consequences in her sorrow-filled eyes.

"Ok." She slides down into the bed. I flick a switch on the wall beside her, and the main lights in the room turn off. The only illumination in the room comes from a bedside lamp beside her. "You'll come back?"

"I'll be back in a little while. Sleep. You're safe in here. Nobody will hurt you."

She shuts her eyes, and I watch her for a few minutes. The feeling of protectiveness I have over her is strange—it's strong for someone I've only known for less than an hour. I need to make sure she's going to be all right, but the only way of doing that is to find out what is going on.

I quietly leave the room and go in search of my father. I find him sitting in the drawing room of the unfamiliar house with the lady who was comforting Joanna earlier.

"Theo?" my father asks quizzically when I enter the room. The woman jumps to her feet and bows toward me even though she doesn't have to. My father dismisses her with a wave of his hand. "I thought you would be resting."

"Not until I know what is going on here."

My father gestures for me to sit, and I do so in the chair vacated by the woman. He indicates to a brandy decanter, sitting on the table next to him.

"I think I'll pass. I've drunk my fair share this evening already, and mixed with whatever you drugged me with, I'll be asleep in a few minutes. I need to know what is going on. I'm married to a woman because it's the only way to save her, evidently. What is going on father? How much trouble are we in? What is happening with Victoria? Is she likely to end up as broken and bruised as Joanna is in a few months?"

"That's a lot of questions." Without lifting his head, my father talks into the half empty brandy glass he's holding.

"That's less than half of the ones I've got floating around in my head at the moment."

"Ok. I owe you an explanation. I had hoped to do it with a fresh head in the morning, but I guess it can't really wait. You remember how I told you I had to give Victoria to Nicholas Cavendish, or he would've destroyed our family name and killed me?"

"Yes." I say, sitting with the foot of one leg resting on the knee of the other.

"Joanna's father was forced to offer her up as well. Nicholas was given five women that night. His right, he insisted, based on years' old rules. I tried to argue they could no longer be valid in this day and age, but I was shot down by those who support his rule. Out of those five girls, only two are still alive: Joanna and your sister. Unlike Victoria, Joanna was not put forward to participate in the trials. Instead, she was sold to a mystery buyer and then disappeared. Victoria's story, you already know. She ended up married to Nicholas, and is now the mother of his daughter. A couple of days ago, my men got word of where Joanna was located. It's been exactly a year ago tonight since we started searching for her. We put together a plan and managed to rescue her."

My father goes silent, and his eyes fill with unshed tears. I know he must be reliving a horrible memory, which he wants to keep buried, so he doesn't have to experience it again.

"She was hidden away in what was little more than a dungeon. No clothes, nothing. The smell is the thing that will haunt me forever: feces, decaying human flesh. Another girl long since passed was left lying there in the darkened room with her."

"What?" I can't quite understand the words I'm hearing. They don't make sense to a brain, which is untuned to such horrors and has been laced with alcohol and drugs.

"It was horrible, Theo. I don't know how she survived. She's so thin. We gave her a steak when we got her back here to try and revive her, but as you saw on the floor when you married, she brought it straight back up. Her stomach is not used to it. We've had a doctor examine her. She's been repeatedly violated. She's not pregnant, thankfully, but…"

My father places his brandy down and slouches forward in his chair. His head's held in his hands, and he's shaking it.

"I'm sorry, son. I'm so sorry. I panicked when I saw her that way. All I could think about was what my own daughter will be going through. I needed to make Joanna safe, and this was the only way I could think it would work."

I slide from my chair and come to sit at my father's feet. It's a position my sister and I used to take when we were younger, and we wanted to offer him comfort.

"It's all right. I understand why. As my wife, Joanna is safe from the Cavendish brothers. You've told me they have eyes and ears in the police, so we can't go to them. Indeed, Nicholas and William are the reason why the police are investigating you for Elsie Bennett's murder. This was the only way of making sure they can't take Joanna away again. We're married, now, and she's safe."

My father shakes his head.

"She needs to be your wife in all ways. If you don't consummate the marriage, they'll figure out a way of annulling it. I know they will."

I hold my hand up to my father.

"I can't think about that yet. After what she's been through, I'm not going to force her into anything."

"You need to bear it in mind though, Theo. They have Tamara on their side with all her fancy education and knowledge. She'll do everything possible to get the girl back for them. William Cavendish has turned her against us. I fear Victoria will never trust us again, either. Nicholas has poisoned her brain, and she doesn't see what he's doing is wrong. I've lost my daughter and her best friend. I can't lose Joanna. She's the only one left to save."

"I know. I'll talk to her. Just not tonight."

My father nods—lines of worry are etched on his face. He's aged so much in the last few months with the stress of everything. I resolve then and there that from this moment on I'll no longer sit back and allow him to take the burden of his fight alone. I'll stand by his side in battle.

"I'm sorry about the drugging. The man who did it shocked me as well. He said it would be the quickest way to get you here, rather than having to take time out to explain it to you. I had to go along with him in the end. I pay him to know what's best in these situations."

"I understand." I've never had any reason to distrust my father, and I won't start now. I'm terrified for the future of our name and the society we operate in, but what I do know is I have a wife now, and it's time to step up and fulfill my destiny.

CHAPTER FOUR

JOANNA

A chill in the air wakes me from my sleep. I pull the blanket farther over my shoulders and nestle down into the comfortable mattress. The sheets feel softer than the ones I'm used to, and the bed's more comfortable, bigger even. Am I dreaming again? It feels so real though. If I had the courage, I would open my eyes and seek the truth, but I'm too scared of what I'll find. As I start to move, one hand brushes against the other, and I freeze when I feel the ring on my left hand. The memories from yesterday are real...they aren't a dream. I'm married to Theo Hamilton. I spring up into a sitting position in the bed and stare down at the antique wedding band on my ring finger. I'm married. Fuck! My head spins again. I didn't die yesterday, but I did fail. Theo didn't sleep with me. I'll be in big trouble.

Looking frantically around the room, I search for a place to hide. If I can't be found, then I can't be punished. No, he'll find me. I tried that once before and was beaten so badly my ribs were broken. But he can't beat me, now, can he? Surely Theo will notice new injuries on my flesh? My head whirls around so fast with all the thoughts running through it. It's like one of those roller coasters at the theme park where your stomach turns on every peak and fall.

Where is my husband? My brain stalls, rapidly braking to a standstill when the thought sparks alive. He should be here? Has he abandoned me already? I jump out of the bed and reach for a dressing gown that's been placed over the back of a chair. Quickly wrapping it around my naked form, I search the room for signs he slept here with me, but there's nothing. Not even discarded dirty laundry from the day before although I can't remember much about what he was wearing, possibly a pair of jogging bottoms and a t-shirt. He's left me already. The Viscount is going to be so angry with me. Maybe I didn't die yesterday, but it's likely I will today. Sorrow fills me up. I wish I could do something right—I'm forever making mistakes. I feel so tired again and crawling back into the bed, I pull the covers over my face. Hiding in plain sight. It's the only option I have left until he comes for me.

I must drift off to sleep, at some point, because I'm woken a little while later to a crashing sound in the room. I jump out of bed and drop to my knees on the floor with my head bowed.

"I'm sorry." Theo comes to stand before me. He offers me his hand, and I stare at it like it's diseased. "I won't hurt you. I just want to help you up. You don't have to kneel for me."

Tentatively, I reach out and taking his hand, he helps me to my feet.

"Did you sleep all right?" he asks, and I just stare at him blankly. This is far too normal. He should be beating me or forcing himself on me.

"Joanna? Is everything all right?"

"You didn't come to bed." I say, looking at the rumpled sheets where I've been lying, alone.

He points at a different door to the main one in the room. "This is an interconnecting room. I slept in there. I wanted to be near you should you need me, but I think you probably need space, for now."

"N-No," I stammer. "You should sleep with me. We are husband and wife. We need to make children."

He laughs at me, and I can't help but feel a little hurt.

"I'm sorry," he apologizes and guides me back to sit on the bed. "I went to speak to my father last night. He told me about your treatment at the hands of the Cavendish brothers. I'm not the sort of husband who would force himself upon you. You need to heal both in body and mind, first."

"But..." I start to interrupt him, and he places his finger over my lips to silence me. I don't flinch at his touch.

"No. We're going to return to London, in a few days. I don't want to leave the estate alone for long. We'll look into finding a psychiatrist and arranging further medical checks for you when we're there. Then, we can discuss the fact we're married. In the meantime, we'll focus on your healing."

I can't answer him. Medical examinations and talking to someone about what I've been through fills me with a terror so great I'm lost for words.

"I've got to head out for a couple of hours. Stay here and rest. Have a nice long bath. Camilla will feed you whatever you want. Don't have anything too rich. I think your stomach is still a little delicate. My father is downstairs if you are worried about anything."

Bile rises in my throat at the mention of his father. Keeping down food, at the moment, isn't going to happen. I just nod. Maybe the time alone will give me a chance to get everything straight in my head? Does Theo truly have no idea what's happening right beneath his nose? I'd like to believe he's foolish rather than compliant with his father's deviances. He's been nothing but kind to me, so far, and to have that illusion shattered would be the final straw to my sanity.

"Do you want me to run a bath for you before I go?" Theo asks as he picks up a set of keys from the dressing table. Is he going to lock me in the room? My eyes flash to the keys and back up to him. "For my car," he reassures and turns his head toward the bathroom.

"Please. A bath would be good," I tell him and slide from the bed. Following behind him as he walks confidently into the bathroom and turns the taps on, I can't help but notice the way his backside fills out the jeans he's wearing. It doesn't mean I want him sexually. It just means I like the look of him. I can look—it's normal. I can be normal.

"Joanna." I startle when he appears in front of me. "I put some bubble-bath in. Are you sure you'll be all right? I'll send Camilla up to check on you in ten minutes." He looks worried. He must be thinking I might drown myself in the bathtub. Little does he know, over the last year, I've had opportunities to kill myself, but I've not had the courage to carry it out. There's something buried deep down inside of me that's still fighting for life.

"I'll be fine. I've not had a bath in a year. Just a shower. I'll enjoy relaxing."

"All right. I'll be back as soon as I can. I'll fetch you some clothes as well." Theo leaves me alone in the bathroom, and the only noise is the gushing of the water from the tap. Padding across the marbled floor, I find a toothbrush and toothpaste laid out for me. I squeeze a little bit of the paste on the brush and clean my teeth. There is also mouthwash sitting on a shelf, and I gargle with that. For the first time in a year, I've had access to a decent toothbrush and paste, and my mouth feels clean and fresh. I stare at the girl in the mirror in front of me. She looks so very different to the one I remember staring back at me before. She looks older, a lot older, with dark shadows under her eyes, skin that's sallow and pale, and a wild mop of frizzy hair on her head. I was an innocent girl the last time I looked in a mirror. I'm a woman now, and a victim. I stand staring until the mirror steams up, and I can no longer see my reflection. Turning around, I catch the bath just before it overflows. I turn the taps off and place a foot towel ready beside the bath, so I don't slip when I get out. I lower my dressing gown to the floor and step into the almost scalding water. Sinking down into the bubbles, I shut my eyes and enjoy this moment of peace and normality. Who knew a bath could provide so much tranquility in a place of such chaos?

"I see you are already acting as lady of the manor." The rough voice of the Viscount sounds from the doorway, and I sit bolt upright. I try desperately to reach for a towel. One part of my brain is telling me I need to get out of the bath and kneel before him, but the other is telling me I'm naked, and he'll see everything. I'm conflicted. I preferred it when I didn't question my training. I choose instead to twist in the bath and kneel for him. Thankfully the bubbles cover my breasts. The Viscount laughs. "I guess I'll accept that."

I don't say anything back to him. You don't speak unless questioned.

"What happened last night? Did my son take you?"

Not the question I wanted him to ask. I can't lie to him. He'll know. He always knows.

"No, sir. I slept alone. He was in the adjoining room."

The Viscount tuts.

"That's not what I wanted to hear. You were supposed to make him want you, using whatever means necessary."

"I'm so sorry, sir. I tried, but he wanted to speak with you, and I fell asleep. He didn't return last night. This morning, I tried again, but he went out. I'll try as soon as he comes back. I'll plead with him." I'm babbling now. Terrified of the punishment, which follows swiftly when my head is grabbed and thrust under the water. I'm held in place as the water fills my nose and constricts my breathing. I try thrashing and pushing back, but I can't free myself. I'm pulled up just as the last of the air in my lungs leaves me. Coughing and spluttering, I try to bring more precious oxygen into my body as quickly as I can.

"I didn't ask you a question."

My head is thrust back under the water, but this time I don't have enough air in my lungs to prevent the dizziness from coming on immediately. When I'm yanked out again, I'm gasping and desperate to breathe.

"You failed me. That means punishment." The Viscount has one hand wrapped tightly around my hair. His other hand goes to his trousers, and he removes his dick from its confines. I'm pulled closer to him, and he pushes himself into my mouth.

"Take it all." He bucks his hips, and there's nothing for me to do but allow him to violate my mouth. "You will do this to my son later. You will allow him to stretch that tight little pussy of yours and fill it full of his cum. You will make a baby boy, and I will mold him in my likeness. I'll make him the greatest heir to the Oakfield Society there's ever been. I'm next in line to becoming the leader of the society, and with William and Nicholas gone, I will get it all." He's thrusting wildly into my mouth—my cheeks hurt, and he's hitting the back of my throat as I gag around him. I can't help being thankful that I've not eaten anything yet. All I wanted was a relaxing bath, but instead, I'm back being terrorized and abused, again. Nothing will change. Ever! I'm to be a human sex toy for eternity. Maybe I should have drowned myself in the water when I had the chance? No! The part inside of me that still clings on to life screams repeatedly in my head, *we are stronger than this...we will survive.* The Viscount buries himself at the back of my throat and with a foul grunt, releases his semen. I work hard to swallow it all when what I really want to do is spit. I did that once and was left unconscious for a few days from the beating that followed.

Withdrawing from my mouth, the Viscount lets go of my hair, and I collapse down into the now cool water as he puts himself away. He then pulls the plug, and as the water starts to drain, he stomps over to the bathroom door.

"I've laid out clothes on the bed for you. Get dressed and get downstairs. You'll be ready to greet your husband when he arrives back. Every time you fail in your task, you'd better be prepared for punishment. You're a whore to my needs... nothing more, nothing less. Don't get illusions of being anything else."

CHAPTER FIVE

THEODORE

I offer Joanna my arm, but she hesitates before taking it. I'd hoped her new found freedom would have helped her find some inner strength and confidence, however, over the last few days she seems to have withdrawn even deeper into her shell. She refuses to sleep alone. She wraps her body around mine, and I've had to tell her more than once our relationship is not sexual. It's as though she's had the need for such things ingrained in her and can't cope without them. We've spent very little time together while I've been busy preparing for our return to London as husband and wife. I made sure a message was sent directly to the Cavendish brothers, informing them I'm back in town, but I haven't mentioned Joanna or even the fact that I'm now married. I didn't hear anything back from them, of course, only a request from Victoria to meet up soon. Although given she's not allowed to visit my home, and I'll be dead before Joanna goes back to Oakfield Hall, I doubt that will happen until after the Cavendish brothers have met their just desserts.

I've spent many hours watching Joanna, wondering what goes through her head. She's panicky, especially when other people like Camilla and my father are in the room. I guess she's not used to being with people after a year hidden away. But she does seem relaxed when she's around me, which I'm pleased about. I'm glad I can make her feel safe.

"Where is your house again?" Joanna asks as the car pulls away from our temporary home. My father has to stay behind in his sanctuary. He's still a wanted man, at the moment, and returning with us would lead to his arrest. I wish he didn't have to stay here and could join us. I feel the weight of responsibility on my shoulders, having to run the estate and look after Joanna. But I know I'm ready for it, and even though it would be good to have him around should I need his advice, I'm certain it's only temporary. He'll be home as soon as we can deal with the Cavendish brothers. I'd been in favor of reporting them to the police, but as my father explained, they have spies everywhere, and it would only lead to more trouble for us than them. Furthermore, Joanna is reluctant to report her ordeal.

I rest back in my chair before I answer her question.

"Just on the outskirts of London. Surrey way."

"How old is it?"

Joanna is wearing a pair of skinny jeans and a t-shirt today.

It's hot outside, the middle of July, and the weather is really heating up. The air conditioning is on in the car, and she's shivering. She's gained a little weight over the last few days, but she's still skin and bones. Reaching over, I hand her cardigan to her, and she smiles at me in thanks.

"It's late sixteen hundred. Nothing too fancy in the grand scheme of things, but it's home. I love the windows. They are massive. The Hamilton family has always been proud, so there was no bricking them up to avoid the window tax like a lot of our contemporaries did in the seventeenth century," I inform her.

"I remember my father telling me about that. We had a couple of the windows blocked up at my childhood home. I always found it strange until he explained."

"Some of the Old English laws are pretty funny, when you think about them?"

Joanna nods in agreement and says, "They are. I did some research after my father told me about the window tax. I'm...I was a bit of a geek for random facts. Did you know it's illegal to carry a ladder on a pavement in the London Metropolitan Police District?"

"Really!" I chuckle at the absurdity of the law.

"Truthfully, well as truthful as the Internet is, every time you see a workman carrying a ladder on a pavement in London, he's breaking the law." Joanna's face lights up, and for the first time since I've met her, I see her smile. It's beautiful. Underneath all the sorrow and fear is an amazing woman trying to get out. "I'm sorry...I'm talking too much." The smile instantly disappears when she catches me staring at her, and she cowers back in on herself as though preparing for punishment.

"No. I like it." I respond immediately, feeling the need to placate her worries. "Tell me another."

"I...I..." She hesitates, fighting within herself to determine what she should do. Then she flicks her head to the side and looks out of the car window at the surroundings. The house we were staying in is far behind us now, and we are speeding down the motorway in the direction of my family home.

"Is it just us going to the new house?" She turns back to face me.

I nod.

"Yes, my father's in trouble with the law. He's wanted on a murder charge. He didn't do it, but we can't prove that yet, unfortunately. Nicholas Cavendish has provided the police with information that somehow suggests my father is responsible. We'll eventually clear his name, and he'll be able to return home. Until then, it'll be just us and a few members of staff at Hamilton Manor."

"Nobody from where we've been staying?"

"Joanna is something wrong? Has someone upset you there? Camilla? One of the guards?"

"*No*," she replies instantly. "It's just everyone there knows what happened to me. What I was forced to do. I'd like to be somewhere people don't know... if that makes sense?"

"Of course." I tentatively reach out and take her hand. I've limited physical contact between us, not wanting to scare or give her the wrong impression, but this feels like the right thing to do. "I understand. No one except me will know what you've been through unless you choose to tell them. Should you need Camilla to visit for some female company, then I'll arrange it. I promise you, Joanna, in my home, you'll be safe. Nobody will force you to do anything against your will."

She turns back to look out the window, and we fall into an easy silence for a few moments.

"Salmon." Joanna suddenly announces.

"Salmon?" I query confused. "Would you like it for dinner?"

"No. It's one of those old laws. You can't handle salmon in suspicious circumstances."

I chuckle at the revelation.

"No dancing around the lounge with a dressed salmon at Christmas then?"

She shakes her head and proceeds to tell me for the remainder of the journey about how beached whales have to be offered to the Queen first.

When we pull up the driveway to my home, I'm relieved to finally be back. I hadn't exactly expected to leave, and a lot has changed since I was drugged and taken by my father. I help Joanna out of the car and show her around the house. I've put us in adjoining rooms again. I know the last few nights I've stayed with her as a comfort blanket, but I don't want to presume anything tonight.

"Do you like it?" I ask as she strokes her hand over an antique dressing table. The room she's in is painted a pale pink with a silk wallpaper hung on one wall. Everything in the room is a family heirloom, including a silver brush and comb my mother used to use, which rest on the dressing table. When she looks out the window, she'll be able to see all the beautiful roses in blossom that Victoria loves so much.

"It's beautiful. I love it."

"I'm glad."

She picks up the silver mirror and stares at herself in it.

"This looks old. You should put it away somewhere safe."

"It's Victorian. From my mother's family. We don't really

have anything to do with them. Apparently, they didn't approve of her marriage to my father."

Joanna places the mirror down and comes over to stand by me.

"Where is your mother? Is she here?"

"No." I shake my head. "Her family were right...the marriage didn't work. She and my father are still married for appearance sake, but they live separately. I don't see her that often."

"I'm sorry. My parents are similar." A sadness crosses her face.

"It's a curse of society marriage, which we won't repeat." The words come out of my mouth before I have a chance to truly think about their implication.

"What do you mean?" Joanna asks, her brows knitting together in confusion.

"That's a matter for a later discussion. As I said, we need to ensure you are healed first."

She turns away from me and looks over at the bed. Her shoulders slump.

"Will you be joining me in here?"

"If you need me, yes. Again, my room is just next door."

"You promise me nobody here knows about me?"

I don't know what propels me toward her, but I suddenly find my arms wrapped around her waist, and her slight body pulled closer to mine. She doesn't flinch but melts into my embrace as though she welcomes the comfort I can offer. With all the abuse Joanna has suffered, alarm bells should be ringing in my head, alerting me to the fact she hasn't run screaming from my touch, but they don't. Instead, I enjoy her warmth against me.

"I promise you. You're safe here. If I'm not around, I will

have a guard with you at all times, so the Cavendish brothers can't get to you. You're mine to protect now, and I will with my life. Trust me."

Joanna goes up onto her tiptoes and presses a soft kiss to my cheek.

"Thank you. You don't deserve any of this."

"Hush." Placing my finger over her mouth, I let it linger there, and she presses her lips against it. There is an undeniable sexual attraction growing between us. For the first time, I start to entertain the thought that this marriage could be more than just a means of offering her protection. I've seen glimpses today of the happy woman she can be. I want more of that. I let go of her and walk to the bookshelf in the corner of the room. Flicking through the titles, I snort out a laugh to myself when I see just the book for her, and pulling it out, I hand it to her.

"Here."

She looks down at it.

"The Guinness Book of Records?"

"I thought you might enjoy it. Considering your passion for random and obscure facts. I'm going to go and make a few calls. You can enlighten me with your new-found knowledge at dinner."

She clutches the book to her chest, a big smile blossoming over her face. I adore that smile. It lights up the room and warms my heart in the knowledge there is hope she can overcome her past.

"Thank you, Theo." She looks down at the book and back up to me. "I'm so glad to have met you."

"Me, too."

I head for the door, but as I reach for the handle I stop, remembering something I need to tell her. As I turn back,

Joanna is settling herself in a comfortable seat ready for a few hours of reading.

"I almost forgot. I've arranged for your mother and father to join us at dinner in a week. They are desperate to see you again."

CHAPTER SIX

JOANNA

"It'll be ok." Theo reassures me with a squeeze of my hand. He's the only person I'll allow to touch me. Yesterday evening, we ate together at the large table in his dining room, and I sat next to Theo while he took his place at the head of the table. At one point, when leaning over to place a plate of grilled chicken, vegetables, and potatoes in front of me, the butler accidentally touched my arm—I immediately jumped up from my chair, sending the food flying across the table and straight into Theo's lap. I was mortified at my own stupidity, but Theo did his best to calm me down. I feel so lucky it's him I'm spending my time with and not his father.

Maybe my stars have changed? It's been a week, and I've not been raped or forced into any sexual act. I feel sort of normal, or as close to normal as I'm ever likely to experience again in my life. I'm anxious, though. I'm so very nervous of meeting my father as I don't know how he'll react, and there's no way of telling. When I was a young girl, he was kind enough to inform me of my fate, which is something I'm aware Victoria's father never did for her. He was also different from Amelia's father because he didn't insist on training me for the trials. I was told what I would need to do but never forced to try them out beforehand. If I wanted to attempt something, it was my choice...but I didn't. I wanted to enjoy my childhood before the inevitable came. Will he be angry at me for not succeeding in becoming Nicholas' wife? He must know it was Viscount Hamilton who bought me, and not Nicholas? Will my father be able to end this charade once and for all? My mind has been filled with tumultuous thoughts all night, trying to envisage all the alternative ways today could go. But every possibility I considered descended into screams when I imagined it was Viscount Hamilton who came to see me instead of my father.

"I promise you," Theo reassures me again as a stray lock of hair falls from the neat French plait I have braided into my long blonde hair, to keep the frizz at bay. Reaching forward, Theo tucks the loose strand behind my ear. His touch is so different to others and sends warmth cascading through my body.

"What if he's angry at me?"

"Angry?" Theo shakes his head in confusion. We're sitting together on a sofa in his lounge. The room is formal in style but with a touch of modernity here and there.

"Because I didn't win? Because of what happened to me?"

I give Theo a couple of alternatives.

"He's your father. He's been worried about you. The second I spoke to him to tell him you were safe and under my protection, he was thrilled. He's been worried sick about your whereabouts over the last year. The Cavendish brothers prevented him from going to the police. He believed you were dead and became a defeated man. I've never heard so many screams of joy when I told them you were safe. It'll be all right. You'll see."

"I know," I reply and find myself leaning into Theo. Am I becoming too dependent on him? I pull away again, but he tugs me back to nestle under his arm.

The door-bell rings, and I almost jump out of my skin.

"I don't think I can..." Getting to my feet, I race for the door, which I know leads me away from the hallway and toward my bedroom. A strong arm wraps around my waist and pulls me into a solid mass of heat.

"You can," Theo whispers into my ear. "I'll be with you the whole time. I promise."

My breaths come out in ragged heaves, but I allow the warmth of Theo's body to bring me comfort.

"You'll stay next to me the entire time? I don't want them to touch me. Please. You have to promise they won't. I can't have them touch me, yet. Please, Theo."

"You have my word."

A knock comes at the door opposite to the one we're currently standing by, and I allow Theo to lead me back to my seat. He settles me down but remains standing.

"Ready?" he whispers again.

"Yes," I reply, knowing I need to face my parents at some point.

"Come in."

I can feel my heart almost beating through my chest as I

watch the door open. It's unhurried and tormenting as if in slow motion like when an old fashioned film breaks. My mother and father enter the room, Edgar and Sarah Nethercutt, the Earl and Countess of Linton. They're still just as regal as I remember. My mother wears a skirt suit in a teal color, and my father is dressed in a formal suit with a monogrammed tie. They look like they are off for an afternoon tea, not meeting the daughter they haven't seen in a year. Theo is wearing a shirt and smart trousers, but I'm just in a long jumper and leggings because I've lost so much weight I don't really fill anything else out. It's easier to hide it this way.

"Lord and Lady Linton." Theo extends his hand out for my father to shake it. My mother lets out a whimpered gasp when she sees me. I can tell she's been crying from the red rims around her eyes—I hate the fact she's upset. She's my mother, and I don't want her to be distressed. She's not a part of this secret society. She's merely an obedient wife who's done as she's been told. Woman have no place as rulers in my world. We are toys to our men's whims.

"Theodore, a pleasure." My father shakes Theo's hand. "I can't thank you enough for what you've done for our daughter."

"Joanna." My mother steps forward and tries to bring me into an embrace, but I shuffle farther behind Theo. I can't let them touch me, and I wonder why? They are my parents—they wouldn't hurt me. Except, that's not true, because my father freely gave me to Nicholas for the sale. He's the reason I've suffered as I have. If he'd left England, taking me and my mother and hiding us away, then none of this would've happened. I drum my fists against my father's chest as the anger bubbling inside me explodes,

"This is all your fault!" I scream with tears streaming down my face. I bash his chest over and over again. All my tension and fear is being dispelled from my body through my fists into bruising punches. Nobody moves for a few moments. I vaguely hear my mother's weeping getting louder, but I'm too focused on the fury seeping from me. Eventually, Theodore wraps his arms around me and pulls me away.

"Enough," he orders, and I bury my head in his chest and allow the tears to soak through into his shirt.

"What did they do?" my father questions, his voice quivering with emotion.

"We don't know the full details, yet." Theo's deep voice rumbles through his chest, and I allow it to soothe me further. "I'm not sure we'll ever know, but the main thing is Joanna is safe."

"And married." my father adds in a poignant tone.

"In name only."—Theodore's voice is tense—"I'll not force her into anything she's not ready for."

"Good," my father answers.

Theodore turns me around, so we are able to sit down together. When I finally lift my head, I notice my father and mother are sitting opposite us. Both have lines of worry etched on their faces. My mother looks older...so much older than I remember her being a year ago. This has been hard on her. She wanted to run away, but it never happened. My head hurts, my body hurts, and I want to go back to sleep.

"Joanna." My father leans forward in his chair. His eyes are full of kindness and love. He's sorry for what happened. I can see it in that moment and let out a whimper. "If I could have changed anything about that night, I would have. You're my only daughter, my little princess, and I love you so much." He stops himself when his voice breaks and takes a deep breath. "I'll do anything it takes to put a stop to your hurt. You have my word. Theo is a great man. I couldn't wish for a better husband for you."

"Thank you." My response comes out like the squeak of a little mouse.

"How do you feel?" my mother asks.

"Good." I find my voice. "Theo has been feeding me well. It will take a while, but I'll be all right." I repeat the motto, which Theo used to calm me down before my parents entered the room.

"You will." Her mouth smiles at me, but it doesn't quite reach her eyes. I know she fears for my mental stability after just witnessing the attack on my father.

The butler re-enters, and Theo looks up at him.

"My apologies, sir, there is a phone-call for you. It's one you really need to take."

The butler taps his hand three times against his leg. It's like a code to convey a message to Theo. He immediately gets to his feet, but I grab his hand.

"I won't be long. I have to take this."

"But..."

"You'll be fine." He smiles at my parents and then looks back to me. "You've got this."

I reluctantly let him go, and he leaves the room. My mother, father, and I sit in silence.

"Theo's a nice man," my mother observes.

"He is. He's being very patient for a man who's suddenly found himself married," I reply and bring a finger up to my mouth and nibble on what's left of my tattered nails.

"Not the Duke but still a catch, I suppose," my father adds, and I open my eyes wide at him. "It'll have to do for now. At least I'll be second in line to the title when we get rid of the brothers. My deal with Viscount Hamilton has gone well." My father gets to his feet and comes to sit on the chair next to me. He brings his arm around my neck and pulls me closely to him. I don't like the touch—it suffocates me and doesn't give me any of the warmth that Theo's does. It freezes me with its icy intentions.

"I've got a message from Viscount Hamilton, my little Joanna. He might not be here with you, but he hopes you are still working hard at your task." He squeezes tighter around my neck. "Given Theo's declaration that he'll never make you do anything you don't want to, though, I think not."

"Edgar, please," my mother begs but is silenced instantly with a furious growl from my father.

"Get Theo's child inside you before the week is out, or there will be consequences, Joanna. Do you understand?" My father is cutting off my breathing now. I can't believe he's in league with the Viscount. I hoped for a father who'd be sorry for giving me away, but no, I have a devil who is still using my body and mind to get his own way. I try to speak, but I can't. I nod my head instead. I know the consequences he speaks of will involve me being returned to the Viscount, and I don't ever want to see him again.

"Good girl."

He lets go of me, and I gasp for air. My heart breaks all over again when I turn to my mother, and she immediately looks away and down to the ground. A true mother would fight for me, but she's too lost in her own tale of sorrow and despair.

"Sarah, it's time to go." My father gets to his feet just as Theo comes back into the room, and I manage with some difficulty to control my breathing in front of him.

"So soon?" A look of concern crosses Theo's face, and coming to my side, he draws me into his arms. I hope he doesn't feel the rapid beat of my heart. It might give away the fact I'm terrified, having finally realized I've no hope of ever escaping the impossible position I've found myself in.

"I fear little and often is going to be all Joanna can cope with for now. We don't want to overdo anything so soon." My father gives me the look of a caring and protective father, but I know differently, now. "I would like to come and see her again in a couple of days if that is all right?" my father asks.

Theo looks down at me. "It's up to Joanna."

I want to scream no. I'm desperate to tell him that I want my father to leave the house and never return.

"Yes, of course," I reply in robotic fashion.

My mother and father take their leave, and I remain alone in the lounge while Theo sees them out. I'm drowning under the pressure placed upon me. I'm breaking with no chance of a reprieve.

CHAPTER SEVEN

THEODORE

I can't help worrying that presenting Joanna as my wife at the society function we're about to walk into is too soon. It's only been a few weeks since my father rescued her, and in the formal halter neck evening gown she's wearing, it's still possible to see how painfully thin she is. Although the deep purple colored gown is designed to hide the scars that litter her back, she's conscious of her appearance and fidgets constantly, which is something society girls are schooled against at an early age. Common sense tells me to turn away from the ornately decorated doors welcoming us into the banqueting hall, but instead, I allow the inherent determination within me for revenge against the Cavendish brothers to take over.

"The Honorable Theodore Hamilton, son of Viscount Arthur Hamilton and his wife Lady Joanna, the daughter of the Earl of Linton," an announcer introduces us, and to an audible gasp, we enter the room with our heads held high. Well, my head is held high—Joanna is trying her best, but the sea of faces greeting her must be daunting. I can feel her body shaking under my touch as I guide her into the room. I take us straight over to an old school friend of mine whose wife I know will be happy to keep Joanna company for the evening.

"Sebastian, Emily," I greet them with a handshake for my friend and a kiss to the cheek for his wife.

"Did we just hear right?" Sebastian asks, a glass of Champagne poised at his lips.

"You did. Let me introduce you to my wife. Joanna, this is Sebastian, an old school friend of mine, and his wife, Emily."

Sebastian leans forward to greet Joanna, but she steps behind my back. My friend eyes me questioningly, and I shoot him a look to tell him not to ask here but to accept it. He does so with a mouthful of Champagne.

Emily waves at Joanna.

"I love the color of your dress. Who's the designer?" I knew my friend's wife would be able to put Joanna at ease. I turn around to bring her back to my side, and she looks up at me as if asking permission to answer the question.

"Freedom, remember," I tell her, and she strokes her hand down the purple silk of her gown.

"It's Stella McCartney. I love her clothes, and Theodore bought it especially for me to wear tonight."

"She's an amazing designer. I've got so many of her outfits in my wardrobe." Emily replies.

A waiter passes with a tray of Champagne, and I take two glasses. I hand one to Joanna, and she looks at it like it's poisoned.

"I've not had alcohol in a year," she whispers so quietly I can barely hear what she says.

"Would you prefer a soft drink?"

She shakes her head.

"I want to be normal. I like Champagne."

"Then drink as much as you want," I say, laughing to try and dispel her tension.

"I'll just have the one." She takes a sip and a big smile crosses her face. I'll need to watch how much she consumes as her body is still recovering and won't be used to the potency of the alcohol, but I'm glad she's trying it, at least for the time being. When I look up, I see the dark fury behind my friend's eyes. He's not stupid and is forming his own opinions as to what has happened to Joanna because it's well known she's been missing from society for a year. My conversation with him later is going to be a very interesting one indeed.

The conversation hushes again when the gong sounds to announce another guest.

"His Grace, Nicholas Cavendish, Duke of Oakfield. William Cavendish, Earl of Lullington, and his wife, Tamara, Countess of Lullington."

The silence is broken when a glass smashes on the floor. I look down at my feet to see Champagne splashed up my trousers and crystal at my feet. I don't need to look up to know it's Joanna who's dropped her glass at the introduction of the new guests. Emily reacts before I do as the crowd goes back to their gossip.

"Oh brilliant, another klutz just like me. I'm terrible. The first time I met Sebastian's mother, I bumped into a table and knocked a family heirloom on to the floor. Ever since then, whenever I go to visit them, they hide anything valuable away." Emily laughs and offers Joanna her hand. "Why don't we go and powder our noses and allow the men to sort this out. Is that all right, Theo?"

Joanna's eyes go wide. She looks between me and Emily, and then across to where Nicholas and William are being greeted by other guests at the party. My nostrils flare with anger. How these two deviant monsters can still be freely walking around when the woman next to me was broken by them is unbelievable? They will get theirs, though, I'll see to that. But not just yet. For now I need to be the strong man I've been taught to be, and pushing all feelings of retribution aside, I need to look after my wife.

"Of course," I tell Emily. "I'll clean my trousers as well."

"I'll join you," Sebastian immediately adds, placing his empty glass on a passing waiter's tray before taking his wife's arm. I bend my arm to allow Joanna to place her hand through mine, and we lead them to the bathrooms as waiters scamper behind us to clean up the broken glass.

"I'll wait here for you," I inform Joanna before Emily takes her a little reluctantly into the ladies' bathroom. Sebastian follows me into the gentlemen's bathroom and does his business as I set about trying to wipe down my trousers. While washing his hands, he raises an eyebrow at me in the mirror.

"So, you going to tell me?"

"It's a long story and not really one for a public bathroom."

He turns the taps off and dries his hands.

"Please just tell me someone else made her as frightened as a mouse? Because you know what'll I'll do if I find out it was you."

"You know I'm not that sort of man." I reply, staring back at him in the mirror.

"Ok, you need any help let me know. She's a good wife for you."

"Thank you," I offer in gratitude to both his comments. "We need to get back. I don't want to leave her alone for too long out there."

He looks at the door, trying to understand my meaning. His mind working over-time, probably trying to link the breaking of the glass with the arrival of the Cavendish brothers. Sebastian is not titled. He's from a rich family who have never been involved in the society from what my father has told me. He wouldn't understand it, and I'm not about to involve him. I fold my arms across my chest in a gesture that tells him he's not going to get any more out of me tonight.

"Ok. It's best I don't leave Emily alone for long, either. She really is terribly clumsy."

We both leave the bathroom, and the first thing I see is Joanna with Nicholas Cavendish standing next to her. Emily's brows are furrowed together in anguish, and Joanna is white as a sheet.

"Get away from her." I stomp furiously across to them and push Joanna behind my back. Nicholas steps away and places his hands behind his back. His nostrils are flared with rage, but I can see he's trying to control it.

"Theodore. Good to see you again … and married? I'll have to inform your sister. I don't think she's aware yet."

"Your Grace," I show him deference to his title and bow. It sickens me, but I'm the better man, and I won't allow my manners to slip. "I'm afraid we've only just returned from the country. I'll be sure to arrange a meeting with my sister, at the first opportunity. I'm surprised she's not with you tonight."

Out of the corner of my eye, I see Sebastian take hold of Emily and pull her closely to him. I nod to him, confirming he's fine to leave, and he leads Emily away. I really don't want to involve him in what's happening here.

Nicholas watches them go before he replies.

"As you know, your sister had a baby just over a month ago, and Rose takes up most of her time at the moment. I'll be returning home to them as soon as possible."

"So you can abuse them like you did Joanna?"

"I'm sorry?" Nicholas genuinely looks surprised, and I can't help but think of him as a fantastic actor. "The only thing I've ever done to Lady Joanna is to brand her, and that was beyond my control. I've not seen her in over a year. In fact, the second I saw she was here, I came to check on her. I'm amazed to find she's married to you."

I snort a laugh at the utter stupidity of his declaration. We all know the truth, so there's no point in lying about it anymore.

"Do I really look like a fool?" I snarl at him through gritted teeth.

"Do I need to answer that?" Nicholas retorts, and my anger flares enough that I ball a fist and prepare to send it flying into his smug rapist face. At that moment, William and Tamara appear, and Joanna grabs hold of my hand before I have a chance to make a show of myself.

"Please," she whimpers with a cry of desperation.

"Ok." I turn to her as William comes and stands steadfast beside his brother while Tamara stands next to her husband.

"Theo, please. Listen to them," Tamara implores.

"Stay out of this," I bark and focus my attention on Nicholas. "Isn't it enough you have taken my sister and brainwashed her? And now you've wound your claws around

Tamara as well. I may have lost them, but I'll not let you take Joanna. You've done enough damage to her. I've seen the scars and heard the screams when she's sleeping. You're sick individuals...both of you."

"Is he nuts?" William exclaims.

"Not now." Nicholas holds his hand up to his brother.

"He must be if he thinks we did that to Joanna. It was his father who bought her."

"William," Nicholas replies tersely.

"Ok. Time for me to do that shut up thing." Earl Lullington folds his arms across his chest.

"Thank you." Nicholas breathes a sigh of relief. "Theodore, I don't know what you've been told, but I've never hurt Joanna, save for the brand. If you just ask her, I'm sure she'll confirm it."

I feel Joanna press closer in behind me.

"Please, Joanna. Victoria desperately misses her brother. She's suffered so much. Now's the time we all need to pull together and support not only her but also help you to deal with whatever you've been through. What I'm trying to do, at the moment, is change the society and make certain there'll be no more sales, and no more demanding of women. This must end. I have a daughter...a beautiful little girl, and I want her to grow up free." Nicholas tries to step closer to us to plead with Joanna, but I hold a hand out to ensure he keeps his distance.

"Enough. Joanna doesn't need to confirm anything to you. I know exactly what you are."

"Let her speak." Nicholas orders with a menacing tone that has several passers-by immediately scatter from the hallway we're standing in. The chandelier lights even seem to shudder with fear.

"He did it." Joanna sobs from behind my back. Her head is

buried in my suit jacket, but she pulls away and comes to stand at my side. "Nicholas Cavendish raped me. His brother watched and sometimes joined in. They do the same to Tamara and Victoria. They've beaten and starved me. They are evil and need to be destroyed."

The hallway falls silent, and I take the opportunity to reform my fist and send it flying into Nicholas' jaw, knocking him off his feet and into his brother.

"Stay the fuck away from Joanna. She's mine, now, and you won't be getting her back. Enjoy the remainder of your freedom because by the time I've finished with you, you'll be rotting in prison for the rest of your lives."

I grab hold of Joanna's hand, and we storm out of the venue and back to the car. I'm itching to return and beat the crap out of the Cavendish brothers, but Joanna's soft whimpers calm my temper. Once we've taken our seat, I bring her into my arms and hold her tightly until she stops sobbing.

"I'm sorry." I kiss the top of her head as the car pulls away, and we commence the journey home.

"Don't be…it's all my fault." She manages to get her words out in between wracking sobs, which break my heart. I vow then and there I will die before Nicholas Cavendish ever lays a finger on her again. This must end. Soon, Joanna, Tamara, Victoria, and Rose will all be free.

CHAPTER EIGHT

JOANNA

The lie that tripped so easily from my tongue last night has haunted me ever since. Thankfully, Theo left early this morning to seek support for what he termed, 'an oncoming battle' with the Cavendish brothers to unseat Nicholas as the head of the Oakfield Society. Theo's father has given him a list of people to canvas, so I'm sure they'll all be people the Viscount has already ensured will support his cause. My father's support of Viscount Hamilton after what that man had done to Victoria, his own daughter, proves to me there are no morals left within the men of the society. I wish I could persuade Theo to leave it behind and disappear to a different country, but I've no chance while he's adamant at clearing his father's name. A name I know is guilty as sin for crimes against me, and I'm pretty sure is equally as guilty on all other charges. Maybe one day I'll be able to persuade Theo of his father's evil actions? But that time is not now. I'm still too scared to tell the truth. The lies are easier since I know I won't be beaten for telling them. It's ironic because in childhood I was punished for the little white lies I told my parents. But these aren't little. They are the sort that could destroy innocent people, and I don't know how to stop them without having to face more of the agonizing degradation of rape and violence I've become accustomed to.

I need to stop thinking this way and start my day. I promised Theo I would try today. Before I was taken, I was learning graphic design in my spare time. I knew I may not have a future so didn't want to specialize, but I enjoyed taking pictures and manipulating them on the computer. Theo asked me the other night what I would like to do, and I told him about the graphics and the photography. The next day, I'd had an all singing and dancing camera delivered to me along with a top specification Mac laptop. I'd also been enrolled onto an online course with the view to doing a degree in graphic design if I wanted too. I was stunned but impressed. I'd spent some time yesterday acquainting myself with the computer, but I want to use the camera today to take photos of the roses in the garden. They really are spectacular and would make a fantastic canvas to work with on the computer.

Retrieving the camera from within the specially laid out cupboard in my bedroom, I check the battery, which is fully charged. I then open the hinged compartment where the memory card is stored and pop a new one in. Theo also bought me several memory cards in spite of the fact each of them probably holds over six thousand pictures, even with high resolution settings enabled on the camera. I'm not sure how many photos he expects me to take.

Placing the camera strap over my neck, I slip on my lightweight shoes and make my way down into the garden. It's a beautiful day, not as hot as it has been over the previous weeks, which is a relief since we're living in a house designed in an era when air conditioning didn't exist. A slight breeze rustles through the leaves of the trees, and I inhale deeply to allow the fresh scents of the garden to settle inside my nostrils. The fragrances are calming and decadent after a year of nothing but four musty walls.

I start walking toward a collection of roses growing over an arbor in the corner of the garden. They are bright red and remind me of blood. Checking the settings on my camera, I look into the viewfinder and start snapping a few pictures. When I'm happy with my first foray into capturing the beauty of the setting, I flick the review mode button on the camera and look at the pictures I've taken.

"Beautiful, aren't they?" The soft feminine voice comes from behind me, and I spin around quickly, dropping the camera on the ground. My heart beats rapidly when I see Victoria standing in front of me, and a memory flashes in my head of our only other meeting. *All of us, in our white linen dresses, standing before Nicholas and the previous Duke of Oakfield while we wait to hear our fate.* She appears to be nothing like the terrified young girl she was back then. She looks glamorous in her tight black jeans and red tunic top. You couldn't tell she'd had a baby only just over a month ago. "The roses are the one thing I miss about this place, apart from Theo of course. I've started a rose garden at Oakfield Hall, but it'll be a few years before they are as beautiful as here. Around by the swimming pool, they are even better. You should take some photo's there."

"What are you doing here?" I ask as I take a few steps back from her. "Nicholas isn't here is he?"

"No. He's not happy I'm here either, but I need to talk with you. We are the only two survivors from the trials, and I need to know what really happened to you. Not the lies you told my brother last night. If Theo is in trouble, I will look out for him."

"They weren't lies," I stutter out before I have a chance to think about what I'm saying.

"Your saying Nicholas and William held you captive for a year, and I didn't know about it?" Victoria rolls her eyes.

"Yes," I try to reply with authority, but I'm shaking so much I have to lean against a nearby bench to support myself.

Victoria rubs her hand against her forehead before stepping closer to me. I jump away from her and find a tree to support me this time, instead.

"I'm not going to harm you. We've both been through enough hurt. I don't know for certain what happened to you, but I know it involved my father. He bought you that day. I saw it with my own eyes."

"No. Nicholas did."

"Joanna, please."

"I need you to leave, or I'll call for help."

Victoria exhales an exasperated snort.

"This is my childhood home. Nobody here will throw me off the premises if I choose to be here."

"Please leave." I muster as much courage as I can and turn away from her and start to walk back to the house. She catches up to me, though, and places her hand on my shoulder. I can't help the scream that escapes from my mouth. "Don't touch me." I push her away but then cower back when I realize what I've done. "I'm sorry. I'm sorry."

We are by the entrance to the house, now, and I flatten my back against the wall waiting for her fury to explode and the pain to start when she beats me.

"I won't hurt you, Joanna. I'm not my father. He gave me away without telling me anything about what would happen to me. Do you know what I went through because of him? I was degraded in front of the society with a scold's bridle on and nothing else. I was naked, and they beat me until I was left unconscious for a few days. I walked across hot coals, and I saw one of the girls put a pistol to her head and kill herself."

I let out a loud gasp and grip tightly to my stomach.

"No."

I want to cover my ears and shut her out. She was hurt, but now she's okay. She's not a broken liar like me.

"Do you know who saved me?" Victoria asks, but I only half hear her, and she knows it, so she grabs either side of my face and forces me to listen. "Nicholas Cavendish. He saved me. He's a good man and is trying to rid the Oakfield Society of men like the old Duke and my father. He's the father of my daughter, and I've left him alone looking after her at the moment. Would I do that if I thought him capable of doing what you accuse him of? Joanna, we can help you. Whatever it is they hold over you, we can put a stop to it and save you. You must trust me. We have to tell Theo the truth. We have to save him from doing something he'll regret in the long run. Please, you have to listen to me." Victoria is pleading her case to me, but I can't do what she wants. I can't. He'll come for me—my father will know and so will hers. They probably know Victoria's here already. I'll be beaten ... raped. I can't. I need the normality of a life with Theo. He's the only one who can take care of me—he's told me as much. I have to support him and what he wants. He's my husband now. He's the only one who can save me, and in return, I'll save him by whatever means necessary—if that requires me telling more lies, then I will. I'll lie to save my husband because he's the only man who's never hurt me. Nicholas Cavendish isn't the good man Victoria is making him out to be. He branded me: he took a red-hot iron and burned his society's crest into my thigh. Would a man trying to put an end to the way his society treats women really do that? Theo can bring the society down. He's the only one. He can get rid of them all, even his father. My brain flits between one fact and another like a washing machine on spin circle. The confusion is rife in my head, but focusing on Theo is the one thing I can do to bring me clarity.

"Nicholas Cavendish and his brother raped and abused me," I tell Victoria.

She lets go of me and steps back, and I see the defeat cascading through her body. She'd expected me to roll over and join her, but I don't know if what she promises is real. *Nicholas branded me,* I repeat in my head to justify my decision. "Please leave."

Victoria nods.

"I'm sorry, Joanna. I didn't realize the full extent of what my father was capable of. He's really broken you. I wish I could save you, but until you realize Nicholas is not the evil in this, there is nothing I can do." A tear tumbles down her cheek, but I turn my head away. I must stay resolute despite the fact a gasp of anguish is caught in my throat, threatening to erupt at any minute. It shouldn't be woman against woman. We are the ones who stay strong and stand together, but not at the moment. We are falling apart because of the society. Victoria continues, "If you ever need me, you know where I am. My door is always open to you."

She starts to walk away but stops.

"I love my brother. He's a good man who knows nothing of what's happened to us. He's the only innocent in all of this. Please don't let it be his downfall. Protect him. Love him. He needs it."

Her heels click along the concrete slabs toward the front of the house. My breathing quickens as they get farther away. A memory hits me of the present the Viscount gave me: the wig made of Tamara's hair.

"Wait." I call, knowing I should keep quiet but unable to silence my tongue from protecting another woman if possible.

Victoria stops and looks hopefully at me.

"It's not what you think. It's just some advice. Watch Tamara closely. I don't know how key she is to all of this, but what he made me do... my captor. His intentions toward her were not honorable. I fear for her safety. Keep an eye on her."

"I don't understand?" Victoria tries to come back to me to ask questions, but I quickly run into the house and don't stop until I'm locked safely in my room.

CHAPTER NINE

THEODORE

The day has been amazing and beyond my wildest dreams. The people I've met on my father's advice have been more than willing to join my campaign against the Cavendish brothers. I feel hopeful we can avenge what they put Joanna through and destroy their stranglehold on the Oakfield Society. As the car pulls up to my home, all I want to do is jump out and run and tell Joanna. She was so quiet after meeting Nicholas yesterday, and I worry intensely it has stirred up all the memories she's tried to bury deep within her. On arriving back home, I allow the driver to open the car door for me, and as I climb out, I see my butler waiting at the front door, holding what looks like Joanna's camera.

"Is something wrong?" I take the steps leading up to the house two at a time, my pulse quickening with worry.

"I don't know, sir. The Duchess of Oakfield visited earlier. Lady Joanna left her camera in the garden when she returned inside shortly after."

I take the camera from him and notice the lens is smashed. In another few quick strides, I've left my butler standing in the hallway, and I'm upstairs and outside Joanna's room.

I knock lightly, three times, before trying the handle. It's locked. Putting my ear to the door, I can hear Joanna crying. Without hesitating I dash quickly into my room and through the interconnecting door into hers. She's lying on the bed curled up into a ball. When she looks up at me, I can see red rims of tiredness and sorrow around her eyes.

"What happened?" I ask as I place the camera on the sideboard and springing onto the bed, I bring her into my arms. She's cold to the touch, so I pull the sheets up to cover her body. "Joanna, talk to me, please."

"Nothing."

"I know Victoria was here. Is she ok? Has something happened?"

"I can't..." she whimpers and then goes quiet.

I pull her farther up the bed, so she has to look directly at me.

"You need to talk to me. I can't help unless you tell me what happened."

She tries to stifle a sob, but it comes out as an exaggerated breath instead.

"Do you ever wonder what it would be like if you were born into a different world, place, or time?"

"Sometimes, but I don't regret the life I live. I know it's honest, and I try to do the best for those around me."

"But what if it's not possible. Because of fear, you're too scared to even think about what the truth is and what lies are anymore. Knowing if you find out what you think is true isn't, then you could be killed for it or worse." I'm deliberately cryptic when talking not wanting to give too much away to Theo. If he discovers the truth of his father's actions, there is a chance he could be killed. I certainly will be murdered for driving a wedge between father and son.

"Joanna, what did Victoria say to you?"

I gently hold her chin with my hand and turn her head from side to side. I'm checking for…I don't really know what I'm checking for, but I have to know she's not injured in any way.

"I want something different," she replies and lifts her head up, so she's looking directly into my eyes.

"What?"

"For tonight. I want to be normal. No hatred, hurt, lies, revenge. None of that. I just want to be husband and wife. We barely know each other. I've told you a handful of things about me. My love for photography and graphics but nothing else. I know so little about you other than you seem to have a passion for philanthropic work."

"But Victoria being here? It upset you."

She shakes her head.

"No. Not tonight. What is your favorite food?"

She shifts on the bed, so she's sitting on top of the sheets. The color returns to her cheeks, giving them a rosy tint. Her eyes are expectant with excitement, and gone is the sorrow and fear that was evident in them before. She has shut away what upset her, and I know I'll never get anything out of her, tonight. In this moment, though, I don't care because I want more than anything to please her and make her happy.

"Filet Mignon."

She rolls her eyes.

"Typical male answer."

I bash my fists against my chest like a caveman.

"Man need meat!" I growl, and she laughs so loudly it fills the room with her delightful sound.

"Woman need chocolate."

She copies my tone while beating her chest.

"I'd never have guessed." I shake my head.

"But do you know how I like it?" she teases playfully.

My brain instantly goes into the gutter, and I imagine her licking chocolate off my dick before I drip the molten delight all over her tits. I'm a hot blooded male, and my wife is sexy as fuck. Not that I'll touch her until she's ready. I compose myself, but I think she's read my thoughts because she blushes.

"With strawberries, raspberries, and blackberries," she quickly adds to dispel all thoughts of my sexual preference for chocolate.

"Nice." I snort a little laugh before reaching out to the phone at the side of her bed and dialing the kitchens. The chef answers straight away.

"Sir?" Despite it being Joanna's room, she'll not use the phone to order anything for herself, so he knows it's me calling.

"Do we have any strawberries, raspberries, or blackberries?" I ask and listen as rustling comes from the other side of the phone while he looks in the fridge.

"No blackberries, but we do have the other two," he replies after a minute.

"Good. What about chocolate?"

"What type?"

"Type?" I query before realizing what he means. I pull the phone down to my chest. "What type of chocolate do you prefer?" I ask Joanna,

"Dark, please."

I nod and return to the call.

"Dark please. Can you melt it and bring some of those small almond biscuits up as well?"

"I'll bring you a chocolate fondue platter, sir. I believe we even have some marshmallows somewhere."

"Thank you."

I hang up and turn my attention back to Joanna who's moved off the bed while I was on the phone and has gone into the bathroom. Despite it only being around seven in the evening, it appears she's changing out of her clothes and into her PJs. I get off the bed and standing casually outside the closed bathroom door, I shout, "Do you like sport?"

"Sorry?" she says as she walks out in her baggy trousers and top. She's as beautiful in her casual clothes as she is in her smart ones.

"Do you like sport?" I repeat and lead her to one of the chairs in the room. She takes a seat, tucking her legs underneath her, and I pull a blanket off the bed and wrap it around her.

"I do." She laughs as though enjoying a private joke, and I cock my head wanting to be in on it. "I was very much into sport when I was younger. My father got really angry at me, at one point, because he wanted me to do hockey or polo, but I wanted to play rugby. He threw an absolute fit one day when I came home and told him I'd made the school's rugby team. It was all right for the boys at the neighboring boy's grammar school to play but not me. I had to quit after a few games, though, having come home with a black eye. It wouldn't have done if any permanent damage had occurred prior to me being given to the society." She falls silent again, and I'm just about to tell her I preferred rugby as a sport as well, when there's a knock at the door. I unlock it and allow the butler to bring in our food. Joanna stands and bows respectfully to him. He repeats the gesture back before leaving us alone once more. She looks between the food and me, waiting for permission to eat, so I nod my head at her. It's the same with every meal even though I've told her she can start eating whenever she wants. She picks up a big strawberry and dips it into the chocolate before bringing it to her mouth and devouring the sweet treat in seconds. I can't help but smile as I watch her.

"How about favorite animal?" Joanna questions me.

"Animal?" I screw my nose up. It's not something I've ever thought about.

"Yes," Joanna continues. "I don't know why, but I've always had a thing for giraffes. I love their faces, and they seem really cheeky to me. They are majestic. It's silly, but I just like them."

"It's not silly. Don't worry. But I don't know about my favorite animal." I rub my chin while thinking. "I like owls."

"Owls?"

"Yes, they're wise, skilled, and can hunt in the dark. A good animal."

"A prowler!" Joanna chuckles and picks up another strawberry. I do the same.

"What about the future?" She sucks on the end of the red fruit.

"What do you mean?" I swallow my strawberry in one bite and choose a raspberry next.

"Do you see yourself as just the future Viscount or something else?"

I breathe deeply and pop the raspberry in my mouth.

"I'm destined to be Viscount. I've seen how my father has run things, and I'd like to do some of it differently, but until I hold the title, I'll follow his rules?"

"What would you like to do differently?"

Joanna sits forward in her chair, listening intently to me.

"You called me a philanthropist earlier, and I'd like to do more of that. Help people who haven't had the privileges in life that I have. Victoria and I said as children we wanted to set up our own art school for people to learn to paint like all the great artists." I go quiet for a moment and remember my carefree sister. Knowing what Joanna has been through, I'm desperately worried for Victoria. I want to get her and my niece away from Nicholas before it's too late, but I fear I won't be able to.

"I promise you, she's happy," Joanna states out of the blue and picks up another strawberry.

"No one can be happy with a man like that. It's delusional."

She looks down to the ground and places the strawberry back on the plate.

"I'm tired. I think I'll sleep."

Looking at the clock, I see two hours have passed with us talking and eating.

"One final question. This time, I'm asking it."

"Ok."

"After this is all done, do you see yourself still being married to me?"

Joanna gets to her feet and comes over to where I'm sitting, opposite her. She places her hand under my chin and tilts my head up toward her face. Slowly, she leans forward and presses a kiss to my lips. It's soft and tastes of strawberries and chocolate. I lick my lips wanting more of her taste.

"You'll always be my husband. You saved me when no one else could."

She goes to turn around, but I grab her hand and pull her back to me. My heart is beating so fast. I've tried to keep my distance from her, not just for her sake but also for my sanity. I must be wrong in the head. She's a victim of abuse and doesn't need me forcing anything on her so soon, but I want her. I want her in my bed, I want my dick inside her, and I want to bathe her insides in my cum until my child grows within her. I've never felt emotions this urgent and overwhelming before. Joanna Nethercutt, no, Joanna Hamilton, my wife, has embedded herself under my skin with her beauty, naivety, and a spirit so strong she could fight a million soldiers single handedly if she wanted to. I stand and pull her to me, so she's resting against my body. My forehead drops forward onto hers and rests there a moment while our eyes look directly into each other's. I shut mine and bring my lips to hers again. This time, it's not a brief kiss but one that seems to go on forever. It grows more and more urgent as every minute passes.

Joanna whimpers under my touch, and I instantly pull back. It's not a whimper of pleasure…it's one of fear, and when I look at her, she has tears streaming down her face. I don't say anything to her—I just swoop her up into my arms and carry her over to the bed where I lay her down and climb in beside her, fully clothed. Then pulling her close to me, so her back is against my chest, I hold her tightly until her breathing evens out, and I know she's fallen asleep. I pushed her too far tonight. I have to be mindful of what she's been through, and how it will shape our future life together. She may never get over it. We may never consummate our marriage, but I'll be beside her like this forever. I allow my own eyelids to flutter shut as the exhaustion of the day washes over me.

The next thing I know, I awaken to Joanna screaming and kicking out in my arms. She's shouting, 'no'. I need to rouse her gently, so holding her tightly, I softly tell her it's a dream, and reassure her I'm here. Eventually she stirs and opens her eyes. They are wide with fear, and there are black circles underneath them where her sleep was disturbed. She pushes me away and sits up gasping for air. Reaching over to the nightstand, I grab a glass of water sitting there and offer it to her. She drinks the whole contents in a few big gulps.

"Tell me..." I try to stop myself from asking because I don't want to upset her any further, but I can't. I have to know. "Joanna, tell me what your dream was about?"

CHAPTER TEN

JOANNA

I've not had a nightmare for a few nights now, and as I struggle to get my breath back, I wonder what triggered it. The day had been intense with meeting Victoria again for the first time since I was sold to her father, but I thought I'd relaxed enough with Theo that evening to overcome my anxiety. The only other reason could be the intense kiss we shared. I know I'll be punished by his father for not taking it further, but something inside me screamed at me to stop. Sitting here now, though, looking at him with worry lines etched all over his handsome face, there's a part of me wishes I hadn't. Because despite everything that has happened to me over the last year, my body is calling out for a normality only Theo can give me. Against all the odds, I know I'm falling for him. He's the man I dreamed of marrying: kind and caring with a serious side but not afraid to laugh when it's needed. When I was a child, and I stood in my mummy's high heels, and my Sunday best outfit pretending to be a bride, he was the man I imagined as my future husband. Fate is cruel—it's given me the man I want, but I know he'll end up hating me because of who I am. Life has kicked me and put me down at every opportunity, and I'm already in hell with the knowledge of what I have to do. That's what I spent most of the afternoon crying about: the fact I have to weave a web of lies because I'm trapped with no means of escape. Victoria loves Nicholas Cavendish. He's not the man Theo believes him to be, but if I don't convince my husband he is, then I'll have to watch Theo die, and I'll suffer more torment at the hands of the Viscount. It's an impossible position to be in, and to make a decision either way curses me forever.

"Joanna, tell me what your dream was about?" Theo asks me again.

"My dream was of the first night they took me. I've not reflected on it for a while now. The memories have become clouded in my head, but the dream was so realistic. The smells of the dark room, the pain as I lost my virginity and suffered a beating." Tears pool in my eyes. I don't want to cry them, though. My tears belong to me, and I'll not allow them to fall for Viscount Hamilton ever again.

Lying back down in the bed, Theo pulls me into his chest, and I lay my head on the smattering of hair there.

"Would you tell me more?" he asks, and my head rises and falls with his breathing as he speaks.

"I don't know if I can." I look around my current bedroom—it's a distinct contrast to the room in which I lost my virginity. This room is comforting and inviting. Somewhere I enjoy lying in bed with my husband. It's nothing like the other room, which was hell. It was dark and had a musty smell. The only furniture in it was a bed and very little else. But that wasn't what I hated the most. It was that I had no sanctuary. Lying here in Theo's arms, I feel safe...but in that room. I knew I could be taken at any moment, and I'd be hurt and degraded.

My mouth opens and shuts like a fish on Theo's chest. I want him to know what I went through, but I'm so scared of reliving it. He tightens his grip on me, and it grounds my anxieties.

"It was a few days after Nicholas had chosen Victoria, Elizabeth, and Amelia to go through to the trials. Daphne had disappeared that night, but I was kept in Oakfield Hall for a few days. I was kept away from everyone else, so they didn't know I was there. One night I was woken up, and a sack of some sort was placed over my head. I remember being bundled downstairs and into a car. We drove for so long, and I had no idea in which direction, or where I was going. I think I shook the entire time. I tried to sing some songs to comfort myself, but nothing worked. Eventually the car stopped, and I was pulled out and led into what I assumed was a house. I remember them pulling the blindfold off my head, and *he* was standing there in front of me like a monster with a devilish smile on his face. I knew then what was about to happen." The memory of Viscount Hamilton's leery face causes me to stop and catch my breath. It sends a shiver down my spine, remembering the way he stepped forward and licked my face.

"Nicholas?" Theo asks.

"Sorry?" I'm so lost in my thoughts I don't understand what he's asking.

"Was it Nicholas or William who took you first?"

The need to lie to Theo sits on the tip of my tongue. If I name his father, it could lead to my husband's death.

"He ripped my clothes from me. I wasn't wearing much ... just a tatty linen dress like the one I married you in. I was naked underneath as had been prescribed for the presentation of the women." I've ignored Theo's question completely, and he seems to accept it because when I pause, he doesn't ask again. "I tried to pull away, to run, but there was nowhere to go. He punched me in the face, not just once but three times. I was barely conscious, which allowed him with his superior strength to hold me down and push roughly inside me."

I stop and sit up, needing to get air into my lungs. Talking about this, recalling the memories and the pain is leaving me dizzy. I'll still not allow the tears to fall, though. I will not!

"Do you need to stop?" Theo sits up and asks.

"No, I need to continue...I was a virgin and wasn't ready or prepared for the intrusion. It hurt beyond anything I'd ever experienced before. It was even more painful than breaking my arm when I was six, and the bone came through the skin. It felt like it went on forever with him inside me, and his hips bucking wildly as I was torn apart down there, but it wasn't really. In reality it was only a few thrusts and then it was over. He emptied his cum inside me, and he made me his whore."

"You're nobody's whore. No matter what's happened to you. Don't ever say that. You're an amazing, strong woman. You're here, having survived all that happened to you, and you're still functioning. You've not shut down to everything around you. It would have been so easy to do that, but you haven't. You've embraced the new life you have here. I bet if I look on your camera I'll see some amazing pictures. Focus on that, and not on how Nicholas Cavendish made you feel."

My heart beats faster while I listen to Theo as he sets me free from the torment of my mind, but then he utters those two words and drags me back into the depths of despair, 'Nicholas Cavendish'. It wasn't a man with that name who did these terrible things to me. It was my husband's father. I'm a pawn in his game, and the whore he made me. I can't fight against what he wants me to do because I don't have the strength any longer. I'm dying inside with no hope of resurrection.

The tears start to fall. I can't stop them. Viscount Hamilton wins.

"Joanna, please. I meant every word I said. You are a beautiful, strong woman. I'm lucky to be married to you. I don't want to scare you, but I've known since the moment I first set eyes on you I wanted more out of our fake marriage than you'd be able to give me. I'm willing to wait forever for you if I have to, but in these few short weeks, I've known you will be my wife not just for the short term but forever. Damn it!" He stops and pulling me toward him, he wraps his arms around me. I can feel his length hardening against my leg, and the significance of it terrifies me but sends shivers of excitement through my body at the same time. I don't understand what's happening. Sex should repulse me. I should want to run from it. I've just told the man holding me in his arms that when I lost my virginity, I was held down and raped. But he still wants me, and I think I want him too. He continues, "I'm sorry...I've never wanted to put any pressure on you. I've only ever wanted you to feel relaxed and happy around me. Get to know me, but I...I need to leave." He suddenly pulls away from me and disappears out of the room before I have a chance to catch my breath.

I lie there for a moment with a torrent of thoughts running through my head. I'm a victim, but I'm not broken. Maybe I can have a normal life? Theo will protect me. Now I'm away from the Viscount, he can't hurt me anymore. I can ruin his plans without him realizing it's me, and if they don't come to fruition, he can't return to Hamilton Manor. I'll be safe forever. As long as he stays a wanted man by the police, I'm safe from him. I can become a wife to Theo. I can learn to love and cherish him— my growing feelings for him tell me that already. I have to go to him. I have to become a woman again and this time properly.

My legs carry me, stumbling, in a dreamlike state through the interconnecting doors of our rooms. My breath hitches when I see Theo, he's lying naked on his bed with his large hands curled around his dick. He freezes when he sees me.

"Joanna, go back into your own room."

I shake my head, telling him no.

"Please," he pleads, but I don't listen and instead take a step closer to him.

"Show me." The words leave my mouth, and I feel like I'm in a dream. I shouldn't want to see him at his most intimate as he pleasures himself, but my heartbeat quickens with the excitement of seeing this stunning specimen before me. *Men are disgusting creatures who cause nothing but pain and suffering,* ...that is what my subconsciousness is screaming at me, but my eyes are telling me something different. They see beauty and the most arousing thing I've ever witnessed. "Show me," I repeat and take a seat on the edge of the bed.

"I don't want to hurt you." Theo's voice is thickly laced with worry.

"You won't," I tell him because I know it's true. I don't know how, but my heart tells me it is, and it's about time I let it rule, at least for a while. My brain has been switched on far too much over the last year. It's time for it to fade into the background and get some rest.

Theo looks between me and his hand, which is still wrapped around his large cock. In my limited experience, it's a thing worthy of display in an art gallery: straight with a large head, and veins protrude along its length, giving it life and presence. He looks toward me again and then slowly starts to stroke himself. His head falls back down against his pillows, and he shuts his eyes. I watch without flinching as he loses himself in the sensations cascading through his body. I've seen a man experience pleasure in sex and ultimately orgasm before, but there is no malevolence surrounding this intimate act with Theo. He's getting off on stroking himself, but it's innocent at the same time. It's not hurting anyone. His eyes screw up tighter, and his body goes rigid moments before jets of white cum shoot from the head of his dick onto his stomach. He opens his eyes and stares straight at me as wave upon wave of orgasmic pleasure hits him. There is so much happiness and delight behind his eyes. It leaves me breathless, and I can't take my eyes from him. I want that: I want that pleasure, that happiness, and that freedom. His orgasm finishes, and the room falls silent except for the sounds of our rapid breathing. Theo reaches over to the side of the bed and retrieves a box of tissues from a drawer. He starts to clean himself off, but I find myself moving closer and stopping him. I then take another tissue and begin wiping him myself. There's a little bin beside his bed, and I throw the used tissues in there. Neither of us have spoken, yet. We've just shared quick glances between each other as I set about cleaning him, and he lay flat on the bed.

"Make me feel that way." I don't realize I'm saying the words until they've left my mouth.

"Joanna?"

I silence him with a finger to his lips.

"Please." Leaning over him, I remove my finger and replace it with my lips. Now, it is my time to fly free.

CHAPTER ELEVEN

THEODORE

My head tells me to push Joanna away, but my heart urges me to bring her closer. *She's not ready*—it's what I keep reminding myself, but with the way she's looking at me right now, I can tell she is. This feels like the right thing to do. How can you fall for someone so quickly when you barely know them? The heart and mind are strange creatures. So often in conflict but ultimately working together.

"I don't want to hurt you," my mind responds, and I pull my lips away from hers.

"You won't." My wife's plea falls from her beautiful plump lips in a breathless moan of need.

"You really want this?" my heart asks, this time, with a quickening of its pace.

"I want to be normal. I've been a victim for too long now. I don't know why, but when you're near me, my heart beats quicker. I need this." Joanna comes at me again and joins our lips together. This time, I don't fight her. I give in to the need surging through me. Despite having come only a few minutes ago, my dick is hard again already, and I want her.

Pulling back for a second time, I rest my forehead against hers.

"If you want me to stop at any point, you say so, and I will. I won't force anything upon you."

"I know," she whispers with a tremble of nervousness mixed with excitement in her voice. "It's why I want to be with you. You'll take me as far as I'm ready to go and not any further. You'll give me what I need because you already know me better than I know myself."

I bring my lips down to hers. My own breath is hitched and ragged with the need coursing through my body. Pulling her over my naked body, I allow her to straddle my thighs. It gives her the control over what we're doing. If I were in her position, I would want to have that.

I'm naked, but Tamara is still wearing her pajamas from earlier. I can feel the excitement between her thighs, and her wetness against my bare flesh. She really did enjoy the show I'd just put on for her. My dick hardens more against her, and I know she can feel the length of me poking into her through her clothing. She's just witnessed the power of an orgasm, and now I am going to use it to show her the pleasure that can come from taking me deep within her...no, not taking, accepting me willingly without pain or torture into her most private place. One I'll never allow to be abused again.

Leaning forward, I run a kiss over her lips and down her neck. Her PJs button up at the front, so while she supports herself over me, I bring my hands up and start to unfasten them. She lets out a barely audible gasp, and her sapphire eyes shift to watch my dexterous fingers at work.

"One." I undo the first button, the bottom one. Moving my hands up, I loosen the second and third in a swift movement. "Two, three."

Joanna's mouth opens and shuts, trying to bring much needed air into her lungs.

"Please," she begs, but I can not allow her fervent appeal to affect the deep-rooted control which is embedded within my psyche. If this were a normal woman I was fucking, she'd already been on her back with my dick pistoning in to her so fast she'd forget what damn day of the week it is. But this is my wife, my delicate flower, and I need to take this slowly so we can both savor every moment of our first time together.

My hands start to shake a little with the need for rigid control, and they fumble over the final button before finally freeing it from its frustratingly difficult small button hole.

Sliding my hands up to her shoulders underneath the cotton fabric of her pjs, I remove her top and drop it down onto the bed. Her breasts are a perfect fit for my big hands. The cuts and and bruises, which had once marred her skin, have disappeared to leave a stunning feminine form. She's everything I could have wished for in a partner. It's as though she was made for me by the gods, not that I believe in that sort of crap. In my opinion, you make your own way in the world, and by protecting Joanna from Nicholas Cavendish, I've earned her love, and her body.

I lower my mouth down to her left nipple—its peak is already taut with the sensations and emotions running through her body. Wrapping my tongue around it, I lavish it with attention while tenderly massaging the other breast under my hand. The pink flesh smells of the lavender perfume she uses mixed with a slight scent of sweat from the day's exertions. It's purely Joanna, unique to any other woman's breasts in my experience. I'm in two minds whether to linger here or travel lower to discover her other delights, but the grinding of her hips against my thighs shows me where she needs my attention.

"I'm going to lay you down. Is that all right?" I ask and then press another quick kiss to her breast.

"Yes." The reply comes quickly, and I place my hands under her hips and adjust us so she's lying flat on her back on the bed. Her eyes are wild with desire but also mixed with nerves. It dawns on me that together we're giving her a chance at a first time, again…although this time it's with her consent.

"Our first time," I moan into her prickling flesh, sucking and savoring her taste as I move down to her stomach and then even lower.

"Our first time," she repeats and wraps her hands around the thick strands of my hair. With a subtle strength, she guides my head to where she wants me between her thighs. Inhaling deeply, I can smell her arousal, and my dick hardens so much I'm certain I could pound nails with it. I need her, but I have to go slow. I think there's only one thing for it. Times-tables. I need to recite them to stop myself from fucking her too hard.

One times one is one. One times two is two. The words are spoken inwardly as I start to lower her pajama bottoms down her svelte legs. She's had no reason to keep herself trimmed, but the hair on her pussy is shaved into a delicate strip. *One times three is three. Fuck. One times four is four.*

Joanna settles herself back on the bed and opens her legs

wide for me. She gives me the gift of her pussy and the numbers in my head go haywire.

Two times nine is sixteen, no eighteen. Fuck.

"Theo, take me," Joanna begs, but I can't answer her. I can't look at her.

"Three times four is...fuck, fuck, fuck, fuck, fuck!"

"Theo, look at me," my wife demands, and the words pull my head up from looking at her perfect pussy to her beautiful face. "Twelve," she tells me.

"What?" I'm confused and shake my head.

"Three times four..."

Shit. I can't have kept my controlling math as deep within my head as I thought I had.

"I'm sorry." I sit back up on the bed. "I'm completely fucking this up."

She snorts a little laugh and then shakes her head.

"No, you're not. You're a smart man and your using your head to make love to me." She points to where my brain is analyzing every minute detail and coming up with the wrong answer. "But you need to use this, instead," she says, placing her hand over my heart.

"I'm so scared of hurting you, though."

"And that's why you're making love to me like I'm broken. I want you to fuck me. Show me how it should be. Show me the feelings I saw on your face when I watched you come. That's what I need, and you're the only person who can give it to me."

I can't help but feel a total loser at her words. So much for being an alpha male. I've been approaching this from totally the wrong frame of mind. Joanna is stronger than she looks. I've told her enough times. If I want her, I should just take her and show her how making love can really be.

I nod slowly at her and tentatively reach out to touch her pussy with my left hand.

She gasps, but it's not out of fear. It's pure wanton desire. I run my fingers over her pussy lips and part them to reveal the delicate bud of her clit hidden beneath. It's peeking out from its hood, needing my attention. With my tongue, I taste the length of her warm feminine flesh. It's pure in its innocence and desire. She tastes like my perfect woman.

Joanna moans and grabs the sheets beneath her.

"More."

I oblige, feasting on her pussy. My tongue tantalizes her clit and then dips into her hole to lap at the essence flowing from within her. She's more than ready for me, but I want to give her an orgasm first. I push a finger inside her. At first, there is a little resistance, but that disappears the second I press my tongue to her clit and flick it.

"More," she cries again, arching off the bed. "Make me a proper woman. Make me normal."

I push another finger inside her to join the one already there and hook them up to rub at the sensitive spot within her. My tongue flicks harder and harder over her clit.

"Oh my god. I'm...I'm.... God."

I use my teeth to nip at her clit, and that is all she needs to fly free, for the first time of her own choosing. A broken angel no longer. She cries out with the pleasure cascading through her, her body jerking as she comes. Her pussy clenches down on my fingers, massaging them with the powerful waves of her first pure, beautiful orgasm. It's the single best experience of my life: watching her find herself. I guide her down after and allow her a moment's rest before withdrawing my fingers and moving up and over her to position my dick at her entrance.

She doesn't need to say anything to me. The look of affection in her eyes is her consent, but she knows I need to hear the words.

"I need you inside me, please." A beautiful melody to my ears that has me slowly pushing into her. Her moist heat embraces my dick within its welcoming haven, and I lose my mind and almost my cum like a schoolboy experiencing his first sexual encounter.

"Now you can use your timetables, if you want," Joanna teases. "I want to come again."

"Bossy!" I laugh and slap her backside. I instantly worry it's too much for her, but her pussy clenching around my dick tells me it's something she enjoyed.

"Don't let me lose you now, Theo."

"You're not going to." I withdraw and then slam back in. Joanna lets out a squeal of pleasure.

"Fuck me." Her legs clench tighter around my body as we settle for the missionary position. The traditional position for a newly married couple. I allow my mind to become lost in the movement between us as my hips thrust in and out of her in a poetic motion designed for only one thing...climax. My eyes meet hers, and the stare between us is intense. It's not just the joining of two bodies but of two minds and souls as well. It's perfect.

My orgasm warms in my lower back, and I know I won't be able to last much longer. Reaching between us, I rub at her clit, and within seconds, she's coming again. Her whole body shatters around me in a violent orgasm of nothing but pleasure and desire. Then my orgasm rips from my balls and out of my dick in an explosion, coating her insides.

Shit! We didn't use a condom. I freeze, and she must realize at the same time.

"I'm clean." I offer immediately.

"So am I. They checked me," she stumbles over her words.

We both fall into an uneasy silence with my dick still inside my wife.

My dick still inside my wife.

I realize it doesn't matter about protection as a vision enters my head of her swelling with my child, and I drop down to kiss her lips.

"My wedded and bedded wife." I chuckle.

"I love you, Theo," Joanna whispers before nestling herself against my neck as I say the words back to her.

"I love you, too."

CHAPTER TWELVE

JOANNA

The world tilts on its axis when the sunlight streams through the curtains, and I realize my husband is not in bed with me. The space where he fell asleep last night is still warm, which suggests he left the bed recently. I listen for the shower, but it's silent. I'm disappointed, and my heart instantly deflates. Was I not good enough for him? Is that why he's not here? Does it show down there I'm a victim of abuse. I want to cry, and the tears well up in my eyes but don't fall when I suddenly notice the time on the beside clock. Eleven in the morning! I don't think I've ever slept this late. No wonder Theo isn't here in bed with me. He's an early riser. My body must have been more exhausted than I thought after our lovemaking. Pulling back the bed covers, my hand slides to my flat stomach. I can't help but wonder if Theo and I created a baby last night. It seems odd to me that by being pregnant I'll be safe from a beating, but equally, I'd love a mini version of Theo and me. A baby to worship and give me hope.

"I'm expecting a child in there as well." The deep timbered voice comes from the corner of the room. It's the voice of my nightmares. Please say I'm dreaming. However, as the owner of the terrifying intonation steps from the shadows, I know it's real. Viscount Hamilton is here. "It's taken you long enough to entice my son into that delightful pussy of yours." The monster comes closer to the bed, and I'm scrambling to cover myself with the bedsheets. I'm back in my pajamas, which thankfully offer me some protection. He's stronger, though, and with a hard pull on the cotton fabric of the sheets, they are ripped from my frantic grasp. "I don't believe this is the way I taught you to greet me!"

Next, I'm pulled from the bed by my arm and thrown onto the floor at his feet. I bow my head and stay quiet even though my entire body is shaking, and my teeth chatter with fear.

"My son is too lax with you. He's always been a softy. Sometimes I think Victoria has more balls than Theo does. Let's just hope what he does have are fertile. This has taken far too long. I'm getting frustrated. Do you know what it's like to hide from the police all the time because Nicholas Cavendish thinks he's found morality? Victoria is wasted on him. It's infuriating!" I jump when he stomps his foot on the floor in protest at his perceived injuries. I know exactly what it's like to be running from someone although my someone isn't the law—it's the man standing in front of me. It's exhausting, debilitating, and so very frightening.

I feel him tangle his hand around my hair before it's pulled hard, so my face juts up to meet his.

"You get a baby in your stomach within the week, or I'll come back and put one in there myself. Do you understand?"

My bottom lip quivers, and I manage to stutter out a, "y-y-yes".

"Good girl."

He bends forward and presses a kiss to my lips. He smells of cigars and brandy—nothing like the fresh and inviting scent of Theo. I want my husband back. Where is he? I say a silent prayer in my head for him to burst into the room and witness his father's abuse of me. My eyes flick to the door, willing it to open and my savior to fill the void.

The Viscount laughs.

"He was called away to a meeting. I'm sure he'll be back later with another vote of confidence in us to take over the society. There are more men like me out there than you'd believe. We aren't all insipid wimps like my son and the Cavendish brothers. We know the real way to treat a woman."

My hair is pulled harder until I'm up on my feet and pressed against his body. I'm so glad I chose to put my PJs back on. Theo wanted me to sleep naked, but I'd told him I wasn't ready for that, yet. I still need the security of my clothing. He helped me re-dress. Maybe if I keep thinking of him, I'll survive what is about to happen to me, and the false hope I had that I was safe here won't be decimated into a crumbling ruin? The Viscount pushes me up against a chest of drawers in the corner of the room. He kicks my legs apart and strokes my pussy through the cotton fabric that's keeping it hidden. 'Theo,' I repeat in my head. 'Remember him doing the same thing. The way he made you feel, the pleasure which cascaded through your body when you came with him inside you.' It's not possible, though. Theo was gentle but dominant when he touched me, having realized I'm not broken. The Viscount, however, is harsh with his ministrations, prodding and poking in a way that's completely devoid of romance and entirely designed to inflict pain. He pushes his finger hard into me with only the linen of my pajamas forming protection from his calloused hand and jagged nails. I can't keep in the whimper falling from my lips, and I hate myself for giving it to him.

"Always the little whore for me, aren't you, Joanna?"

He thrusts his fingers in a couple more times before withdrawing them.

"You know, when this is all over, I think I'll keep you for myself. My perfect toy who'll take anything I can give her. My cock really enjoys your cries. It makes it so hard."

He grinds his hips into me, and bile rises into my throat at the thought of what he can do with his repulsive member.

"Now is not the time for frivolity. I'm here for one reason alone."

The Viscount finally allows me to breathe by putting some distance between us. I gasp air into my lungs and adjust my pajamas to make my aching private parts more comfortable. That will have to do until I can burn my clothes and shower in scalding water to make myself feel cleaner. I'll never be able to feel completely clean again, though.

Turning around, I watch the Viscount open up a briefcase I hadn't seen before. I don't even want to begin to guess what he has in it, but I know it won't be good. Nothing with this man is ever right. How can I have gone from feeling confident in myself again and strong enough to make love with my husband to having it all destroyed in a matter of minutes? The realization dawns on me there will never be any escape. This is my life until the day I die. Theo may be adamant he'll protect me, but the problem is he's protecting me from the wrong enemy. The burden weighs heavily on my shoulders, and I sink to the floor.

Viscount Hamilton looks at me and shakes his head with a look of disgust on his face.

"Weak... just like all women."

He pulls out an envelope from his briefcase and stomps menacingly back over to me. I cower away, wanting to crawl into my own skin and hide.

"I've already told you I don't have time to play today. You can stop with the whimpering act. I need my dick inside you to make that fun, and I'm only here for this."

He throws the envelope down in front of me.

"Well open it!" he shouts, and it sends a shudder all the way through my body.

My hand tentatively reaches for the envelope, and I open it as quickly as I can while fighting to control the terrible shake coursing throughout my body. I pull something out and notice it's a photo. I instantly recognize the person captured on camera. It's a younger Nicholas Cavendish, and in his hand is a painting. It's vaguely familiar: the vibrant yellow flowers punctured by the glowing red blooms of two poppies. It was in Oakfield Hall. I remember it from the day I was sold. Victoria was staring at the picture for ages, and I wondered why. I never had a chance to ask her, but I've since learned from others she has an appreciation for art.

"I don't understand," I mumble and then shrink back scared I may be punished for talking.

"You don't need to understand. All you have to do is give that to Theo."

I look down at the picture again. It gives me an unsettled feeling in my stomach. Nicholas is dressed head to toe in black, and the outfit he is wearing is not the clothing of someone who'd be carrying a priceless painting around for any honest purpose.

"It's stolen." The words escape me, and I will my mouth and brain to disconnect. If they keep speaking my thoughts, I could really end up beaten or worse.

The Viscount laughs out loud, the sound filling the room.

"Maybe you are smarter than I gave you credit for." He takes the photo out of my hands and places it back in the envelope. "Of course it's stolen. How do you think we all have the money we do? Looking after old houses and maintaining certain social standards doesn't come cheap. Nicholas Cavendish thinks he can give these things back and get away with it... No, it's not happening."

My tormentor kneels down in front of me and runs his tongue over my face.

"Art equals money. Money equals power. Power equals women, and women equal slaves. That is the future of the Oakfield Society."

A final kiss is pressed to my lips, and I'm thrown onto the floor before the Viscount leaves me lying there, alone. My heart pounds in my chest—its rapid beat is loudly thumping, and I place my hands over my ears willing it to go away, wanting the world to go away. I'm never going to be free. I slide my hands down my body to my stomach.

"Please God, don't let a child be in there. I can't bring another life into this world. It's corrupt and evil. It's hell. Hell is on Earth, and the devil is Viscount Hamilton."

CHAPTER THIRTEEN

THEODORE

I throw my car keys into the pot on a table in the entrance hall where I keep them. Today has been a complete waste of my time. A wild-goose chase around most of London with little result. My first meeting didn't bother to show up, no doubt paid off by the Cavendish brothers, and my second one disappeared halfway through when I mentioned I was married to Joanna. I've no idea what his problem is, no doubt something to do with her father. I've been doing some research on Earl Linton, and it seems he's not as innocent as he makes himself out to be. I wonder if Joanna is aware he was once arrested for rape, but all the charges were dropped when the victim was found dead. A rather convenient death he couldn't be linked to, so he got away with the whole thing. I think I'll keep a better eye on him. It's crossed my mind before he could be a spy for the Cavendish brothers. The last thing I need is for them to know our plans before we're in a position to implement them.

I need to lose the tension in my body, and my beautiful wife is the only person who can do that for me. I didn't like leaving her still sleeping this morning. I wanted to wake her and take her again, but she looked so serene and peaceful, curled up in a little ball, so I decided not to disturb her. I start for the stairs leading to our bedroom, and taking the steps two at a time, my cock hardens with every step.

"Theo." I spin around when I hear my wife's voice coming from behind me, and in no time at all, she's in my arms, and I'm pressing my lips to hers.

"I missed you." I can't help but notice the way her body tenses, and how her eyes fail to meet mine. "What's wrong?"

"Nothing." The answer is quick, probably too quick.

"Joanna, is it about what happened last night?" My cock rapidly deflates at the thought it was too much for her, and she's suffering because of me making love to her.

"No, no. I promise you. I'm a little sore, but it was perfect." She shuffles her feet on the floor still looking away from me.

"Then look at me and tell me what's the matter because I know something is?" I place a finger under her chin and tilt it up, so I can meet her sapphire eyes.

"I made something for you, but I'm not sure if you're going to like it."

Cocking my head, I raise a suspicious eyebrow.

"What is it?"

She holds her hand out.

"This way."

Following Joanna through the house, she leads me to the busy kitchen. Staff are running around preparing dinner. The mouth-watering scent of roast beef wafts in the air, and my stomach rumbles. If I'm not going to be having sex with my wife, anytime soon, then a roast dinner is the perfect way of relaxing me, especially if it comes with a full-bodied red wine and Joanna at my side.

"Where are we going?"

The staff get quickly out of our way as Joanna leads me into the part of the kitchen that's used for making sweet confectionery. Sitting on a table in the middle of the room is a cake.

"You made me a cake?" I question.

"Yes, it's a Dorset apple cake…my grandmother's recipe. The chef helped me a little bit as I couldn't remember a couple of the processes, but it's been so much fun to do. It felt normal."

I press a kiss to her forehead in gratitude.

"It looks beautiful. Am I allowed a slice?"

"Of course." Joanna reaches forward and pulls a knife from next to the cake and cuts me a large slice. She places it on a plate and hands it to me. My butler enters the room, at that point, with a cup of what appears to be tea in his hand.

"Lady Hamilton insisted this is the best tea to drink with her cake." He places the tea down, bows, and leaves.

I bring the slice of cake to my mouth and take a bite. The apple, cinnamon, and crisp sugar topping elicits a moan of pleasure from my mouth.

"It's delicious." I take another bite and then a sip of tea. "Perfect."

"You really like it?" Joanna stands hopeful on her tiptoes.

"Don't tell the chef, but I think it's better than his cakes."

I give her another kiss to the forehead and quickly wipe away the crumbs I leave there.

"I loved making it with my grandmother. It was something I liked to do whenever I was upset. It's normal, so very normal, and it's just what I need before…" She shuts her eyes when she says the final words. I put the half-eaten slice down.

"Joanna, please tell me what is wrong? It's not just the cake is it?"

She inhales deeply and reaches for an envelope on the sideboard.

"I should have given this to you sooner. I brought it with me when I was rescued." She hands me the envelope, but the shake in her hand tells me something isn't right here. She's keeping something from me. I'm not sure what. I open the envelope and am greeted with a picture of Nicholas Cavendish and a painting. My father told me the society was famous for stealing paintings to fund its activities. If this is what I think it is, it could be the key to bringing down the current leader of a corrupt society, making it good again.

"Joanna, do you know what this is? Is this the only copy?"

She nods and then shakes her head.

"Yes. It's Nicholas with a stolen Van Gogh painting. The photo implicates him in the theft of it. I had another copy made this afternoon. It's stored in my room."

"It does incriminate him. I need to think." I start to pace the kitchen area. My head tells me to take this straight to the police and have him arrested, which would be the best way of bringing him down. But my heart is telling me to use it to do the one thing I've wanted to do from the start, and that is to ensure the safety of my sister, my niece, and my sister's friend, Tamara.

"What are you going to do?"

"I should take it to the police?"

She nods at me.

"You should, but you're not going to, are you?"

I pick up my slice of cake and take a final bite before heading for the door.

"Go up in your bedroom, lock the door, and don't answer it to anyone but me."

I don't wait for an answer. I know she'll do as I ask. Instead, I grip the envelope tightly to my chest and make my way through the house, grabbing my keys from where I threw them earlier and go back out to the car.

It doesn't take long for me to travel across London and into the suburbs, heading for Oakfield Hall. It takes even less time for me to be given an audience with Nicholas because I storm straight past his butler and into the current Duke's office. He is alone and looks up from a pile of paper with a frustrated expression on his face.

"I guess I shouldn't expect you to have the manners of good breeding, considering who your father is," he sneers at me and stands up. "What can I do for you brother-in-law?"

The words linking us together as family have me stomping across the room and pounding a fist into Nicholas' smug face.

"I'll never be a brother to you in any way, shape, or form. You disgust me. I'm here to put an end to your hold over my sister and Tamara, and in doing so, protect my niece."

Nicholas rubs at his cheek where I hit him but doesn't go down or attempt to retaliate. Instead, he looks tired and bored with the conversation.

"How many times do I have to spell it out? I'm in love with your sister. She's chosen to be with me and willingly given me a child. I've put your sister on a pedestal and will worship her forever. I'm not the evil man you think I am. You've been severely misinformed, and if only you'd listened to your sister, you'd understand that."

I cut him off,

"I'm not going to listen to lies instilled into her with violent beatings and rape."

He grabs my shirt.

"I've never once taken your sister without her consent. You need to listen to yourself. Your listening to the diatribe of a man who gave his daughter up to be abused by a society full of corruption. I'm putting a stop to that. Together with your sister."

I push him away forcefully.

"You expect me to believe all that when I have to listen to Joanna screaming and crying every night because of what you and your freak of a brother did to her?"

Nicholas has been calm until now, but my mention of his brother and the stigma that's been attached to him since birth sends him into a rage of monumental proportions. He lunges at me, and despite dodging him, he catches me in the stomach with a winding blow. I cough through the sudden pain and launch myself back at him in a flurry of fists.

"My brother is different to the norm, but he isn't a freak. It's a medical spectrum."

We trade blows as we continue to shout at one another.

"And my wife is forever damaged because of what you did to her."

"I didn't touch her! I didn't buy her that night."

"No, you got one of your old pals to do it instead, didn't you? Not satisfied with having one woman you wanted them all."

"When are you going to shut up and start listening? It was your father who bought her."

"Liar!"

I send a harsh punch into Nicholas' face, but it misses at the last minute when I'm pulled away. Spinning around, I find William glaring at me.

"You need to listen to him," the younger brother spits out and let's go of me to stand tall beside his brother.

"I don't need to listen to either of you. I've got all the proof here I need to destroy you." I pull the picture from my pocket and hand it to Nicholas. He goes pale and hands it to his brother.

"It captures your good side at least." William shrugs, and Nicholas rolls his eyes.

"This isn't what you think it is."

He looks across to the picture.

"So, it's not you stealing one of the world's most expensive paintings by a very famous artist. One that was stolen in 2010 and has only just been recovered. In London, incidentally."

"He's got you there," William informs his brother.

"Not helping at the moment," Nicholas responds through gritted teeth.

William rolls his eyes and takes a seat at one of the desks.

"All right, it is me who is stealing the picture, but I was also the one who gave it back. I was told to steal it during my father's rule, and at that time, I didn't disobey him.

I shake my head, not believing a word coming out of this man's mouth. I doubt he even knows what is right and wrong anymore with all the lies he's spinning.

"You've got twenty-four hours to have Victoria, Tamara, and Rose delivered to my house with all their belongings. After which time, you and your brother will leave London and never contact them again. If this doesn't happen, I'll be sending this straight to the police. Your reign of terror is over."

"I'm not giving my wife up." William jumps to his feet, and still holding the picture, he rips it up.

A malevolent chuckle escapes my lips with triumphant glee.

"If you think that's the only copy, then you're not as bright as I've been led to believe."

Turning back to face Nicholas, I stare him down,

"Twenty-four hours. The clock is ticking."

I don't wait for a reply. I simply turn on my heel and leave to return home to Joanna. Soon my sister and Tamara will be free. I know my father would have wanted me to use the ultimatum to take over the Oakfield Society, but the safety of Victoria, Tamara and Rose is more important. I'm sure he'll understand when I tell him.

CHAPTER FOURTEEN

JOANNA

I know Theo told me to go to my room and lock the door, but I can't. A heavy knot sits deep in my stomach. Guilt weighs heavily on me. I don't know for certain what he's doing at the moment, but I know it will involve his sister. He cares deeply for her and will use the evidence I gave him to fight for her. But I can't help fearing that he's rescuing her from the good and drawing her back into the path of evil, especially when his father finds out what he's done. I've made everything so much worse, but what was I supposed to have done? Everything is a horrible mess. I need space to breathe and to clear my head.

I race back through the kitchen, not stopping to talk when a few of the staff ask me if I'm all right. Running up to my room, I retrieve a pair of sandals and a cardigan and put them on, then grab a small handbag I know has some change in it. Theo gave me a mobile phone the other day, but it has a tracking feature in it. Not wanting to be followed, I leave it behind. Making sure the coast is clear, I leave the house by the front door and escape down the long driveway before anyone can see me.

My pulse is racing the entire time. I can't believe I'm being so bold. What if the Viscount finds out and comes after me? Is he watching the house? My eyes dart around me, making sure I can't see him anywhere. I should go back. This is foolish. No, I'm a strong woman. I can do this. I keep walking, and with every step, I'm led farther away from the house. My pulse starts to slow, and I feel normal—if normal is measurable anymore.

The sunlight of the warm September day beats down on me, and tipping my head back, its rays illuminate my pale skin. I'd almost forgotten how bright it can be when the sun shines. Darkness has consumed far too much of my life recently, and it feels good to have a little light in it. Light like I experienced when making love to my husband and feeling complete for the first time. Sadly I was only dreaming when I thought it could lead to a happily ever after. That's not in my future any time soon – probably never.

"Heh," a masculine voice calls out, and following its deep tones, I see a man and woman embracing in the street. He's dressed in a smart suit and carries a briefcase. He looks like he's just come from work. The woman is pushing a stroller with a child sucking on a bottle of milk sat in it.

"I can't believe it!" the woman exclaims with excitement. "How long must it have been?"

"At least five years," the man responds. "I think the last time I saw you was graduation day. My god, I was so drunk at the end of that party. Did you see Timmy Collins? He was dancing on the table with the dean's wife."

"I remember that." The woman laughs. "He was so drunk. I think there was talk of taking his degree away from him straight after the incident."

They both laugh louder, and the child looks around to see what is capturing his mummy's amusement.

"Yeah, I think he kept it in the end. Along with the dean's wife. They are married now and have a son."

"Really?"

The man nods with wide-eyed delight. Just then the child drops his bottle onto the ground and begins to grumble. Bending down, the man picks the bottle up and hands it to the woman who thanks him. She sucks on the nipple and gives it back to her child who mutters something that also sounds like a thank you in baby language. My hand instantly goes to my flat belly, and I repeat the silent prayer to keep me from falling pregnant until I can find a way out of the mess I'm in.

"Who's this little one then?" the man asks.

"This is Jamie. He's three next week."

"Three. Wow. Big boy!" The man ruffles the top of the little boy's head, but Jamie's more interested in draining his bottle of all the milk. "I see a lot of you in him. I bet his father likes that. I know I've always wanted to see a lot of my wife in any children I have."

The woman's expression changes, becoming dark and furious.

"He wouldn't know. I caught him sleeping with my best friend the week after I found out I was pregnant, and I've not seen him since. I told him about Jamie, but he isn't interested. It's been a nightmare trying to get some child support out of him."

"Jerk!" The man shakes his head, and his face turns red with anger. "Some men shouldn't be allowed to become fathers." He looks up to where a small café is situated. "Look, can I buy you a coffee, and the little mite a biscuit or something?"

The woman takes a second to answer. I can see her weighing up her options of returning home to what is probably a lonely house with nobody but her and her son, or enjoying the company of another adult for a little while longer.

"Yes, why not."

The man motions for her to go first, and I watch them a little while longer until they disappear into the café. The two of them hadn't seen each other in a long while, but the bonds of their friendship have lasted, and I'd like to think they'll catch up with each other and not lose touch again. There has to be some hope in this world.

A scream off to my left captures my attention, and I start to watch another couple. A man dressed in a tatty T-shirt and ripped jeans is holding a woman by the throat and is shouting obscenities at her. The woman is dressed in jeans and a tunic top, and her pink, orange, and blue hair is scraped back in a pony tail, but as she pleads with him to let her go, it starts to come undone. I take a step closer to them, feeling an insane urge within me to help her. But my heart is racing, and gripped with fear, I'm unable to do anything. Instead, I become rooted to the spot and watch like a voyeur as the scene evolves. I'm not the only one, though. Others around me stop and stare while some continue walking by and even step into the road to get past them. No one goes to help the woman.

"You fucking whore! How long has he been sticking his filthy dick in your cunt?"

"Listen to yourself, Damien. You've gone insane. I've never once slept with your brother. I'm your girlfriend, for crying out loud."

"I'd believe my own brother over a skanky piece of dick warmer like you. He said you like it up the ass, and I know just how greedy you are when it comes to anal."

The woman tries her hardest to escape from her captor, but he has her too closely held around the neck.

"I can't breathe."

"I should snap your fucking neck."

"You wouldn't." The woman's eyes go wild with fear. "The baby, Damien."

I hadn't noticed before, but the woman's stomach is swollen large with a child growing inside her.

"What? A cracked-up bastard. I've got no idea whose piece of shit your growing. It could be anyone's. If you've opened your legs for my brother, then I want to know who the fuck else you've fucked?"

"No one. It's your baby," the woman screams, and the man slaps her hard across the face. Her lip splits open, and blood starts to drip from it. An elderly gentleman steps up to the couple. I want to tell him not to approach them because I know what could happen to him, and to her for that matter, while this man is so angry. An angry man is a dangerous thing. My mouth opens but then closes again without saying a word. Tears pool in my eyes, and I need to look away, but something forces me to keep watching. It's like a car crash on a motorway:

you need to concentrate on the road, but human nature forces you to look at the devastation.

"I think that's enough." The elderly gentleman tries to stand up tall.

"Fuck off, grandad," the angry man spits at him. "Or you're next."

"Damien!" The woman screams and squirms, her hair flopping all over her face.

"You need to step away from her," the older man continues, but Damien's had enough, and letting go of his partner's throat, he wraps his hands tightly around her multi-colored hair and yells, "I said stay the fuck out of it." He then balls his fist and sends it flying into the face of the elderly gentleman who immediately drops straight down onto the ground and lies there unmoving. A few of those watching scream in shock but no sound comes from my mouth. I've seen men like Damien before. He's nothing but a bully. Sirens wail in the distance, and the woman's still screaming. Damien lets her go and disappears down the street as fast as he can.

"Stupid old man." The woman spits blood onto the unconsciousness form on the ground. "This is all your fault. If he gets arrested, I'll find you. Next time, mind your own business."

The woman takes off running, just as a police car grinds to a halt at the scene. I can't watch anymore. To go from seeing a man so kind and friendly toward a woman and child, and then to witness violence so extreme and unnecessary, leaves me conflicted about the world. Maybe it isn't just me who experiences the hell I'm in? In a bit of a daze, I stumble farther along the street. If the first woman has lost her man, could she find happiness with another? Her old friend, maybe? What about the second? Will she continue to be blinded to the truth about the man she insists is the father of her unborn child? Or is she what Damien said she was? A 'crack whore' who will destroy the life of the child growing inside her. There are always two sides to the story. Heaven and hell.

Someone bumps into me, and I stumble back.

"I'm sorry." The man reaches out to grab me before I fall. My skin heats, and I can feel the palpitations starting. He's touching me. Is he going to hurt me? "Are you ok?" The man's brow furrows, and he looks at me with genuine concern. I can't speak to him, though. I need to put distance between me and him. I push him away and start to run. I've lost track of where I am, and nothing looks familiar. Why did I do this? I wasn't ready. I need to rid myself of the evil stalking me at every turn before I can try to be a normal person again. I'm the only one who can put a stop to this.

In the distance, I'm relieved to see a phone box. They are few and far between on English streets nowadays, and I pray this one is working. Retrieving some coins out of my bag, I feed them into the slot and lift up the phone. It has a dial tone, and I breathe a sigh of relief. My fingers hesitate over the buttons when I realize I don't know the number to Theo's house. Damn it. Why didn't I bring my phone? There is only one number I know: one I had drilled into me since an early age, should I need it. I don't want to call it because I know it'll lead to trouble, but maybe I could use it to my advantage? I need to be smarter. I need to be stronger. I need to be the old Joanna, not the victim of abuse I've become. I dial the number and wait for someone to answer.

"Hello." The deep masculine voice booms down the phone when the call is connected.

"Hello, Daddy..."

CHAPTER FIFTEEN

THEODORE

"I can't believe you've been so stupid. What were you thinking? Actually, don't answer that. I don't think you were thinking. Well, not of anyone but yourself." The angry masculine voice comes out of my lounge as I walk in through the front door.

My stomach is sore from the fight with Nicholas, and I'm sure he got a punch in that will leave me with a black eye tomorrow. All I want to do is go to bed and not have to deal with more hassle. I nod at my butler with a request to let me know what's going on.

"Earl Linton, sir."

"Joanna's father?" I query with bewilderment.

"Yes. From what I can gather, Lady Hamilton left the premises without means of communication and got lost. Thankfully she had some money on her and was able to remember her father's phone number."

"She did what?" I hiss.

"She left the house, sir." My butler cowers down at my sudden angry outburst.

"And you let her?" I stand up tall against him. I'm furious knowing Joanna was out there alone, and at a time when Nicholas Cavendish is probably baying for blood.

"I'm afraid she was rather sneaky in her ability to dodge those watching her."

The angry, raised voice comes again from the lounge, but this time accompanied by a sorrowful whimper from my wife. I loom large over my butler.

"Then you'd better remind everyone that Lady Hamilton does not leave this house without a guard. If it happens again, I'll be looking to change my staff to a set who can follow orders."

I don't pay my butler any more attention. My fury is now focused upon my wife for putting herself into such a dangerous situation. If she thinks the telling off she's getting from her father is harsh, then she's in for a big lesson once I start on her. My heart is beating so fast. Why would she be so stupid? I pound my way across the marbled floor, my dress shoes resonating in a series of eerie clicks. Thrusting the lounge door unceremoniously open, I stomp into the room, and with a growl, I start to admonish my errant wife.

"Is it true?"

Joanna and her father both freeze and look at me with wide eyes.

"What?" her Father stutters at me. The look of concern in his eyes draws me in, and I can't ignore the uneasy feeling I'm getting in the pit of my stomach, telling me he's worried about something other than a daughter with no regard for her own safety. He's like a deer caught in the headlights. I'm about to question his reaction when Joanna steps in.

"I'm sorry." She comes closer to me, and I'm drawn into the sadness in her eyes. "I was stupid. It was such a foolish thing to do. I would have been all right, but a man bumped into me, and I lost my sanity a little."

My anger begins to dissipate, and Joanna's fresh lavender scent calms me. I pull her close and press a kiss to the top of her forehead.

"Did he hurt you? I'll find him."

"No. It was an accident. I wasn't really looking where I was going." Her eyes glass over momentarily, and I know there's more to this story than she's telling me. I won't push her here and now, though. Alone, later, is a different matter. She corrects herself by taking a deep breath and breaking our eye contact. "I promise I won't do it again. I just wanted to experience freedom, having not had any in ages."

"You'll never have it while the Cavendish brothers are breathing," Earl Linton interrupts with his matter of fact response. I'm so captivated by Joanna's beauty I'd almost forgotten he was in the room. She weaves a spell around me and draws me completely into her love.

"She'll be safe soon. The Cavendish brothers will be out of London in twenty-four hours."

"What?" the Earl responds, looking confused.

"Joanna provided me with a piece of information, which will secure the freedom of my sister and niece along with that of Tamara, their friend."

"Freedom? Information? I don't understand. What have you done?" he shouts at his daughter who steps closer into my side, her hands shaking.

"Calm yourself in my house, sir. I won't have you shouting at my wife like that." I place myself between father and daughter as I vent my growing frustration that a good day, which was developing into a triumphant one, is now looking like it's shrouded in more issues.

"I want to know what is going on? If this involves my daughter and can come back on me, somehow, then I need to be informed," the Earl demands.

"It will not reflect on you," I interrupt. My anger previously soothed by my wife is now growing again at her father's arrogance.

"Will you just tell me what is going on?" Earl Linton slams his fist on a table. It rocks, and the glass ornament on it crashes to the floor.

"Calm down!" I yell and motion with my eyes to the smashed glass. "I'll allow you one breakage, but anymore and you start paying for it."

He looks to the floor and then back up at me.

"That piece is of no value anyway. It's fake."

It's my turn to breathe deeply and control my temper. I turn my back to Earl Linton and focus my attention on Joanna.

"Do you want to go upstairs while we finish this conversation?"

She shakes her head and reaches up to my sore eye. I flinch a little when she touches the sensitive flesh.

"You're hurt?"

"Nicholas is worse." I smirk but stop when she steps back horrified.

"This is all my fault." Joanna's eyes start to blink rapidly. It's like she's trying to understand something that will never make sense. Her breathing accelerates.

"Joanna!" her father barks from behind me, and she looks up at him with so much horror in her face. I'm beginning to wonder whether the fear she feels for the Cavendish brothers isn't only the result of what they did to her but also due to her father's treatment of her whilst growing up.

I turn back to him.

"Did you abuse her?"

"What?" he spits at me.

"As a child, did you hurt her?"

"Never. What do you take me for?" The Earl folds his arms across his chest and resolutely stares me down. "I think you owe me an apology. I would never touch my own daughter."

I back down immediately. My senses tell me something is wrong, but apart from the issue with the alleged rape of the woman who died, I've never heard anything to question Earl Linton's abilities as a father.

"He sold me…" The words come from behind me. They are spoken so fast it takes my brain a few seconds to register them. "For cash, I don't know the exact amount, but it was thousands. He got thousands for me being sold."

Joanna slaps her hand over her mouth when she's finished her accusation. My mind is still struggling to take it all in. It's like I'm wading through deep water with heavy, bulky clothes, weighted down from the saturation. I open my mouth to speak, but her father beats me too it when he lunges forward and wraps his hands around his daughter's throat.

"You lying little whore." He shakes her, and I can only watch on as my brain struggles to catch up with what I'm hearing and witnessing.

"It's true," Joanna gasps. Her whimpers of pain penetrate

into my subconscious, and I grab the Earl by the back of his collar, and with almighty strength, I send him flying across the room and into the wall.

"Tell me again." I stand large over Joanna, my breathing quick and my fists clenched hard.

"W-w-what?" she stutters between hitching in gasps of air. Her father had been holding her so tightly around her neck that already a red ring of inflammation has appeared.

"Say...it...again," I repeat slowly, every syllable pronounced with meticulous precision and definition. I don't want my meaning to be misconstrued in any way.

"He sold me for money. I wasn't given away because my father was forced to. He received payment." Her words are equally as clear. I've learned a lot about her since we've been together. The way her eyes flick with darkness at the corners when she's hiding something—a lie hidden within a story. There is none of that this time. She's being as honest now as she was when she told me she loved me. It's the truth. My nostrils flair, and Joanna sinks down onto the floor.

"Please," she whimpers, and I nod once to her before turning rapidly and once again grabbing her father who has only just begun stumbling to his feet.

"You're never welcome in this house again. If I see you anywhere near my wife, I won't hesitate to kill you." I send a fist flying into his face. He's an older man and not built to withstand my assault. He staggers backward, and his eyes roll in his head before he comes back to his senses. My fury increases, and I send another two punishing blows to his face. His nose cracks, and blood splutters out over me. "You will stay away from everyone we know. You will not move in the same circles as me. You will have Joanna's inheritance plus any money you received for her put into her account before the month is out, or we will report this to the police. And..."—I pause for dramatic effect—"I will find some way of bringing back the previous rape charges against you, and if I have to, I'll plant evidence of you murdering the girl as well."

The Earl who is barely conscious manages to take in what I'm saying.

"There's no proof," he responds, spitting blood in my face.

"I'll make some."

He starts to laugh and looks over my shoulder to Joanna.

"I hope you realize what you've started. The apple never falls too far from the tree."

I've heard enough. I send another quick succession of punches to his face, and he slumps down unconscious on the floor.

Joanna whimpers quietly on the other side of the room with her arms wrapped around her, cradling herself in comfort.

"Theo."

"Did he ever touch you?" I ask and step over the prone body, currently bleeding over the priceless oriental rug my father always loved, but I couldn't stand.

"No. I promise you."

"He just sold you."

She nods and looks down at her feet.

"Head up," I order, and she immediately responds. Tears are streaming down her face now. She's breaking down in front of me. The shell she's erected around herself to keep in all the real truths of the situation is crumbling.

"More," I demand, but I know instantly from the frightened expression in her eyes I'll get nothing else out of her at the moment. With a blink of her eyes, she shuts down again. I move beside her, and my arms snake around her waist, pulling her into me and the inconveniently timed erection, which juts from my trousers. I can't explain it, but protecting my woman has left me needing the softness between her thighs to counteract the violence of my acts. I have to know she's not going to fall apart at revealing the truth about her father. I need her to know I trust her implicitly and believe in her honesty. My lips press down onto hers in a passionate kiss, which is as intense as the emotion that flooded the room when she spoke her fateful words. I need her, and I want her, but not here. Bending down, I scoop her up in my arms, and we leave the violence of the lounge behind us. I'm heading for the stairs when my butler appears.

"Will the Earl be staying for dinner, sir?"

I snort a laugh. I can't help it. By morning, my bruised knuckles may be as sore as the black eye given to me by Nicholas Cavendish, but I'll never regret inflicting them on my father-in-law.

"No, he won't," I respond to the butler as Joanna buries her head in my chest, her warm breath tickling the skin under my shirt. "I've left some trash in the lounge. Please see it out and ensure it never returns to this house again. If it does, kill it!"

CHAPTER SIXTEEN

JOANNA

I can't quite believe what I just did. I allowed those words to fall from my mouth, condemning my own father. Half a million, that was what I was sold to Viscount Hamilton for. My father wouldn't have received all that money. A fair chunk would have gone to Nicholas' father, but my own would have been compensated well for having a failure as a daughter. He's out of my life, now, but I know I've started a chain of events that could lead to chaos and death. Strangely though, I don't fear death—it's the lies that terrify me more. I don't want to be a part of them any longer.

Theo carries me up the stairs, two at a time, and deposits

me tenderly on my bed. His face is splattered with blood, but I don't find it unattractive. It gives him a look of danger and power.

"Are you all right?" My husband kisses my lips and down my neck. I welcome his affections. I want him, need him. I feel strength for the first time in ages, and it ignites flames of desire within my body. It would be dangerous to think this will all end well, but for now, I'll embrace my new-found courage.

"Take me," I plead on a breathless whisper as my tightly coiled body unfurls and welcomes my husband between my thighs. He continues to kiss lower until reaching my breasts, and his hard length presses into my leg as the excitement within him builds. My back arches, wanting to draw him in closer. I need him now... no more waiting or thinking about it any longer. I second guess my decisions too much. I need to go with instinct.

"Theo, please."

"Patience," he replies, and then taking the shirt I'm wearing in his hand, he rips it open, sending the buttons popping and flying around the room. "I'm going to savor my wife. And only take her when I think she's ready." His large hands encase my breasts, and he squeezes hard. It sends a pulse of energy straight down to my clit, and I can feel myself getting wet as I prepare to take him when he's ready to give himself to me.

"Need you naked," Theo growls, helping me to sit up while removing what remains of my shirt. Next my jeans are quickly discarded along with my underwear. "You have perfect breasts." His hands slide around my back and unclasp the fastening of my bra. It's pulled off and thrown across the room, landing over an antique lamp on a dressing table where it swings back and forth. "Damn." Theo sits back on the bed, stroking himself over his trousers. His knuckles look sore. The bruising I can see is the result of the words I spoke earlier, at least in part, when I condemned my father.

I lean forward and gently press a kiss to each of the cuts on Theo's hands. The metallic taste of his blood gives an erotic edge to the vision in my head of me kissing away his injuries. He's protected me more than any man has ever done before. He twists one of his hands around my hair and pulls my head up so our mouths can meet. They combine in a tumultuous tango of emotion and lust, crashing together like rough seas breaking over land. I'm tasting him: his masculinity encapsulated in a spicy mixture of the scent of oaky wood aftershave and the flavor of coffee…his favorite drink. This is my Theo, my husband.

He pushes me down until I'm lying on the bed and looks at me again. When my eyes follow his hand as it travels over the contours of my breasts, I see blood is smeared onto my skin from his shirt and face.

"Never again." His vow needs no explanation. I know he means my father will not be allowed to harm me again.

He shifts from the bed and quickly removes his clothes. His hard cock springs from the captivity of his trousers with an excited bounce, glistening already at the head with pre-cum. He strokes himself a few times before lying back down on the bed.

"Up," he orders, and I willingly obey my husband. From under my hooded eyelids, I look up at the intensity in his face. His commanding presence framed by the soft lighting in my bedroom. He's pure sex on legs with a strong jaw, deep chestnut eyes, and full lips swollen from our passionate kissing. He reaches out and wraps his hand around my hair before pulling me down so I'm level with his dick.

"I want you to suck me."

I hesitate momentarily, but it's enough to worry my husband. He immediately releases my hair and brings me up to lie against his chest.

"I'm sorry. You don't have to."

"I do," I respond into the small covering of hair there. "I want to. I have bad memories of oral, but I want to replace them with good. Just like I replaced the vision of losing my virginity with our first time."

"Joanna."

I free myself from his embrace and move back down, so I'm lying next to him on the bed at his groin. I slide my tongue over his body and toward his dick. Little nips with my teeth ignite his flesh, and I can feel it heat to an inferno.

"Fuck!" he exclaims out loud when I wrap my hand around his dick and bring it to my mouth. My tongue darts out and licks up the salty taste at the tip. There is something intrinsically masculine in his flavor. He's nothing like his father or any of the other men I've been forced to service before. He's sweeter, fresher, cleaner, perfect. I swirl my tongue around the tip a few more times before drawing it into the warmth of my mouth.

"Fuck." Is the only word Theo appears to be able to utter at the moment because as I draw him in farther the expletive is repeated a few more times. "Fuck, fuck, fuck!"

Circling my mouth around his length, I draw him to the back of my throat. I was forced by his father to deep throat. The first time, it scared the life out of me, but with Theo, I'm not afraid. I want to please him. To show him I'm here for him only. That I'm not a damaged soul, but the sexual goddess of his dreams when I allow myself to live.

I swallow his length and hold him there for a few seconds

before pulling back and expelling his length from my mouth. Saliva drips from my chin as I repeat the process accompanied by a loud moan of pleasure from my husband. I can feel my own excitement drip from between my thighs. My clit thuds with its own need. I'm getting excited from pleasing a man and making my husband happy.

Theo jolts me away from his dick.

"I'm going to come if you carry on doing that."

"Then come," I purr, having newly found the sex kitten within me.

Theo laughs. "There will be plenty of time for that another day. For now, I need in your pussy. I want to be immersed in you and pumping my hips so hard you're screaming my name as you explode underneath me."

I let out my own little laugh at the mild-mannered gentleman, and his dirty sex talk. I think I'm not the only one finding their inner self in this relationship.

"Do it then," I offer and lie back on the bed. He places himself at my entrance and pushes straight in, in one long thrust before settling and allowing me to adjust to his intrusion.

"Wet as always. Are you like this whenever I'm around?" Theo rubs a finger over where we join. He then captures my legs and pulls them up to rest on his shoulders so he can drive deeper within me.

"I have to go and change my panties whenever you walk into the room."

"I think you should just stop wearing them. I can have you whenever I want, then."

"I'll hold you to that if I do."

The bantering between us is carefree and easy. It's a normal couple in love. That's what we are. Here and now, we are free from all the oppression and fear created by the Oakfield Society.

Slowly, he starts to move, and the mood between us shifts. Our playfulness dissipates, and silence fills the room with the seriousness of what we are doing. We are making love. My legs are lowered to the side of his thighs, and we settle into a missionary position, Theo's eyes meeting mine as we move as one. We have years ahead of us to explore the many different ways you can have sex.

"Tell me what really happened the night my sister was taken to the society." Theo leans forward and presses a kiss to my lips as he breathes the words into my mouth.

"I can't." A single tear falls from my eye and weaves a path down my cheek. I want to tell him and end all of this, but the fear within me is still ingrained. I'm not ready to jump over that final hurdle yet.

"I'll protect you. Nobody will hurt you."

"You can't protect me from the monsters you can't see."

"What does that mean?"

Another tear falls, and I shut my eyes as Theo continues to undulate his hips, thrusting in and out of me.

"Joanna."

"I love you," is the only reply I give before an orgasm bursts out of me from nowhere. It erupts deep within me and cascades through my body with a powerful surge of pleasure. I'm shuddering and shaking underneath him. I'm calling his name and milking him to his own orgasm. His affirmation of the love we share is spoken on a final groan as his cum explodes into my inner warmth.

We both go still and silent. The sounds of our rapid breaths the only noise filling the room.

"Theo."

He pulls out of me and gets off the bed. His shoulders are slumped, and he looks defeated. He's no longer the tower of strength I rely on to protect me.

"If I go to Victoria, will she tell me the truth?"

The question causes my breath to hitch. It's not something I've ever really thought about. I thought he would have already asked her, and she would have told him. I just thought he didn't believe her because he thought she'd been influenced by Nicholas.

"Haven't you spoken to her before about the night she was given to the society?"

He shakes his head and looks down at the ground forlornly.

"I think I feared the answer, and then later when she tried to tell me, I chose to believe her mistaken. I was convinced she'd been brainwashed by her husband."

I can't believe the words I'm hearing from him. The walls he has built, based on a solid belief in what is right and wrong, are breaking down around him. I should open my mouth and tell him it was his father who bought me, but I can't. I try, but nothing comes out. In the end, I pull the sheets up around me and curl into a ball in the bed.

"Go to her, Theo. Listen to her. She's your sister. She can tell you what I'm too scared to admit. She's the only one who can save us, now."

CHAPTER SEVENTEEN

THEODORE

I make sure Joanna is safe when I leave her alone, this time. She's sleeping in our bed with the sheets tangled around her as the early morning sun floods in and illuminates her now flawless skin. I've given her the means to protect herself, if necessary, with an illegal hand gun next to her bed. Before leaving, my father gave it to me as a means to protect myself after Elsie's death. Joanna's from an upper class family, so I've no qualms about her knowing how to use it. It's the sport of the elite to shoot small discs for fun. She'll be more used to a shotgun, but the principle is roughly the same. Instinct will kick in should she need it. I know most people would say I'm insane to leave a weapon with a victim of the horrific abuse she's suffered, but I know she's free from most of the torment from her bad memories. I don't fear her hurting herself, even for a moment. Silently creeping from the room, I leave my butler instructions that no one is to leave or enter the house while I'm absent. Nobody at all, no matter who it is. At this point in time, I don't know who I can and can't trust any more, but something in the lines of worry crisscrossing his face tells me this gentleman, who's been with me for most of my life, will protect my wife. He's aged as much as I have over the last few weeks.

It doesn't take me long to return to Oakfield Hall. It's early in the morning, and the streets are still empty. The imposing gothic style manor sends chills down my spine. This place holds so many dark secrets, which those around me seem to be a part of while I've been kept in ignorance. Or has it been that I've not wanted to hear the truth? No matter what the reason is, I need to know, now. I need to discover what is really happening around me, and what type of pawn I've become in a game I fear is about to turn deadly. My sister according to Joanna is the only one who can give me answers. I need to listen to her.

I knock loudly, and a butler appears at the door.

"I'm sorry, sir, but you are no longer welcome here," he informs me and makes to shut the door. I place my foot across the threshold just in time and curse when the heavy wood slams against it. Damn, English oak! That's going to hurt for a while.

"I want to see my sister."

"She doesn't want to see you. Please move your foot, or the consequences will be upon your own head."

"Victoria!" I shout through the crack in the door. I can just about see my sister on the stairs behind the butler. Nicholas is standing beside her with his arms wrapped around her. His face is as bruised as mine feels.

"Go away, Theo," she informs me with a voice I can hear is close to cracking.

"I need to speak with you," I shout back.

"I'm not leaving Nicholas. You can do whatever you want with that picture of him carrying the painting. We'll fight you every step of the way." Her resilience breaks on the last word, and a whimpering sob fills the cavernous hallway.

"Leave," Nicholas orders with murderous tones.

"I need the truth," I try one last time. "I need to know what happened the night our father gave you to the Cavendish family." Victoria's hand flies to her mouth, and she bends over sobbing, trying to bring air into her lungs. Nicholas rubs her back. "I know Joanna's father was paid money to give her to the society. I know I'm being lied to, Victoria. I need the truth no matter what it is." I pause, my vehement pleas for information are leaving me exhausted. "I want to save my wife. I love her."

Nicholas waves his hand at a butler, and the door opens.

"You'll listen to her?" He steps toward me as I'm admitted into the hall.

"I just want the truth. No more lies. Joanna is terrified of something. You, I think, but I'm not certain." Confusion laces my tone. "All I do know is I want to protect her, and she tells me my sister is the only one who can help me do that."

"I'm not going with you, Theo," Victoria repeats. "You say you love Joanna. Well, I love Nicholas. He's not the monster you think he is. What I have to tell you is going to hurt. It's going to destroy you."

"I'm ready." I take a step closer to my sister and hold my

hand out to her. I can tell she's been crying for hours. Her eyes are red-rimmed, and she looks exhausted as if she hasn't been sleeping and not only because she's the mother of a newborn.

With some reluctance, Nicholas lets Victoria go, and taking my hand, she leads me into the lounge where I assaulted her husband earlier.

"Do you need me with you?" Nicholas looks terrified to let her out of his sight.

"I need to do this with Theo on my own. We are at fault for not telling him sooner. I wanted to protect him from the truth, but he's become embroiled in it anyway. We need to do this as siblings together."

"I'll wait outside. Leave the door open."

She nods at him, and we enter the lounge. She leads me to the sofa, and we sit on it. Her hands feel cold, and I wrap mine around hers to warm them.

"I won't leave him, Theo. I love him in just the same way as you love Joanna."

I look at the door where Nicholas stands guard while we converse. He looks tired. His demeanor does not appear to be that of a man who is filled with confidence in regard to his power nor does he seem capable of being the demon I've been led to believe he is. His look is that of a man who's frightened of losing his wife and daughter. The truth finally dawns on me. Nicholas acts exactly the way I do when I'm around Joanna. His eyes always light up when Victoria is with him. He's protective of her but only because he loves her.

"He loves you, too." I turn to my sister. "I see it now. Victoria, you have to tell me what happened. I can't be kept in the dark any longer. When I married Joanna, I was brought into whatever fight it is you're embroiled in. I'm confused, and I don't know what the truth is anymore. All I do know is my wife is terrified, and I can't protect her unless you tell me. Please."

"It will hurt, Theo."

"I'm ready. Tell me what happened the night you were brought here."

She shuts her eyes,

"I want you to listen to everything, please. Before you speak, you have to listen."

I nod acceptance of her terms.

"Father came and found me the day I was given to Nicholas. He told me it was time for my debut in society. I was dressed by Elsie in a white linen gown, and she styled my hair in a French plait."

"A white linen gown. Joanna wore one to our wedding." I realize I've interrupted her already and bow my head in apology.

"We all wore them…five girls in total. All born during the same year, and all given to Nicholas on his thirtieth birthday"

I nod because my father has told me about this being a requirement of a centuries old society our ancestors were forced to join.

"I was led into the room and introduced to another couple of the girls. I remember Joanna well. Her father was telling her off because she had frizzy hair. She looked terrified. I, on the other hand, was confused. I didn't really understand what was happening. Eventually Nicholas and his father appeared, and we were brought forward one by one and branded with the Oakfield Crest."

Bile rises in my throat. I've seen the mark on my wife's thigh: a vicious scar in the shape of an Oakleaf.

"After that, everything became crazy. We were lined up and inspected by Nicholas. He was told to choose three of us to carry on further in the trials to select his wife. The other two would be sold."

"Trials?" I ask, and she nods, and then looking sorrowful, she lowers her head.

"I endured some of the trials, and they've shaped me into the person I am today. Nicholas seems like a bad man when I tell you all this, but he isn't. He was under the influence…no, the control of his father. I saved him from that, and he saved me in turn."

"What trials?"

"Theo, please."

"What trials?" My response is terse, my hands pull away from warming my sister's, and I clench them into fists.

"I was placed in a scold's bridle, for one, before I was led around naked while being whipped."

"A scold's bridle?" I can't believe I'm hearing this from my own sister. She's suffered just as much as Joanna has, possibly even more. What type of people do things like this in modern society? What type of organization is the Oakfield Society? "Who did this to you?"

She looks up at her husband, and I don't need her to answer. I know exactly who it was. Without another thought, I'm out of my chair and racing across the room with my fists held up high in front of me.

"Theo, no!" Victoria screams. "Please."

My fist is inches from Nicholas' already bruised face when I pull it back before landing a punch.

"You monster. How could you do that?" I spit at him.

"I regret it every day," he responds, and I see the guilt in his eyes.

I spin around, pulling at the ends of my hair in frustration.

"He did that to you, yet you love him?" I can't understand

my sister's reasoning, and I'm doubting her sanity at this point. Has she been brainwashed? "Does he still hurt you?"

"No." Victoria is on her feet and pleading with me to understand. "Never. He's not the man he was that day, and that's why we're being attacked. He's trying to change the society from what it once was and eradicate the evil element within it."

"The artwork?" I question.

Nicholas responds, "We are returning it all. Since the inception of the society, art has been stolen to fund it. The eldest son of the leader is taught the skills needed to continue providing for the society. I stole the painting, but I also returned it along with several others."

"So, you're a thief and an abuser! Yet my sister says you're a good man."

"He is, Theo. He's the best. He's trying to make things better, but he's being thwarted at every turn."

"I'm not buying this, Victoria." I reply, shaking my head. My skin heats with fury, and a bead of sweat forms on my brow. "He's not a good man."

"Nicholas may have done wrong. He'll pay in eternity for some of the things he's done, but he is a good man in a society full of evil," Victoria hisses at me through her clenched jaw.

"Evil…that's all I keep hearing from you, but the only evil I see is him."

She shakes her head and slumps back against a table. "That's because you are too afraid to look closer to home."

"What's that supposed to mean?" I query, fearing the answer.

"Our father." Victoria replies.

It's my turn to shake my head in a furious denial.

"He saved Joanna from Nicholas."

"No, Theo. Nicholas never had Joanna. Remember I told you two girls weren't chosen and were sold instead. Joanna was one of them. The night after I was given to the Oakfield Society, Joanna Nethercutt was sold to our father for five hundred thousand pounds. The day you introduced her as your wife was the first we'd seen or heard of her in over a year."

"No. He took me to her in the middle of the night and said the only way to save her was for me to marry her."

"It's all part of whatever plan he has to take over the society." Victoria holds her hands out to me, willing me to believe what she's saying.

"No." I'm done listening to their lies. My father's a good and honest man. He'd never do anything like this. He's been trying to save Joanna, not hurt her. "I'm not listening to this anymore. It's all lies. Nicholas has brainwashed you. You've admitted yourself that he paraded you around naked and had you beaten. He's the bad man, not our father."

"Theo."

"No." I push past Nicholas and into the hallway where William and Tamara are waiting. Tamara holds a pile of papers in her hands.

"Out of my way," I tell them, but neither move. Instead, Tamara steps forward and hands me a printout from an ancestry website.

"Remember you did a DNA test once, hoping to find a link to royalty? I know you didn't find that, but you did discover a link to a half-sister."

"Not this again." I throw the paper on the floor not wanting to hear her fabricated tales of how we are brother and sister. It's nothing but lies designed to ruin my father's reputation.

"Your father raped my mother, Theo. He killed her, and when I get the proof, I'll see him rot in jail."

"Lying bitch."

"It's the truth." William bends down and picks up the paper. He holds it directly in front of my line of sight, and I can clearly see the results identifying Tamara and I as half brother and sister.

"This is fabricated."

"I'll do a proper DNA test with you, if you want?" Tamara offers.

"No!" I shout with fury.

"Theo, please listen. You promised me you would. I know you love Joanna, and we are just trying to save her. She and I are the only two of the five girls left." Victoria places her hand on my shoulder. "Please, listen."

"I can't." I'm shaking so violently now. It's too much to take in. Tamara is my half sister. My father bought my wife for five hundred thousand pounds.

"Show him." Nicholas steps around to stand next to Tamara. She still holds one piece of paper in her hand, which she offers to me, but I'm too scared to take it.

Nicholas continues, "Your father is no longer Viscount Hamilton. He desires a greater title. My own. One which my death would lead to under the terms of a treaty he and my father signed before my father's death." Nicholas takes the paper from Tamara and thrusts it into my hands. I look down at it. The words blur, and I struggle to read them, but gradually the truth finally sinks in. My father is the man behind all of this. He's lied to me from the start. Nicholas Cavendish never abused my wife. He never had her, but my father did all along. The words become clearer on the page, and I'm able to see my name identified as the current incumbent of the title of Viscount Hamilton.

"I'm the Viscount?"

"Yes." Tamara nods. "I've checked the documentation twice and had a friend check it as well. It's all legally binding."

"I don't understand why? If he's after your title, why give me this and not tell me?"

Victoria wraps her arms around me, and I allow her sisterly affection to calm the confusion I'm feeling.

"He's setting you up, brother. He's given you his name to take the fall for everything."

I open my mouth to speak, but I can't.

"Do you know where he is, Theo?" Nicholas asks me, and all I can do is nod. "Then you need to go to the police and tell them."

"I'll come with you," Victoria offers.

"I will as well," Tamara also confirms.

The shock of everything finally overwhelms me, and I drop to the floor. Victoria comes down with me and cradles me in her arms as I struggle to get breath into my lungs. I'm trying to understand everything I'm hearing. From the foggy haze of my brain, only one thought emerges though. If Nicholas Cavendish didn't rape and abuse my wife, who was it? I don't really need to ask myself that question though for I already know. It was my father.

CHAPTER EIGHTEEN

JOANNA

I know the instant I wake Theo isn't in the bed with me. He's gone to see Victoria. I'm sure of that. Part of me is terrified at the thought of him finding out the truth, but the other part rejoices in the fact we could be at the end of the torment. Is it possible to dream of a life outside of the dictatorship of Viscount Hamilton? Could it be a reality? What if Theo doesn't believe his sister? What if the words my father spoke about the apple not falling too far from the tree are true? Have I been blindsided all along, and Theo's in league with his father? My heart aches at the thought of that. I don't want to believe it as the truth. I'm a good judge of character.

Surely, he's the kind and protective man I've fallen in love with. The thought I might have got him wrong sends a shiver down my spine, but I dismiss it as quickly as I think it. No, I trust my husband. He'll come back and save us from the nightmare we've found ourselves engulfed in. A war between members of a society we know little about. How can it be that an agreement made between a group of gentlemen in the eighteen hundreds has defined my future in such a violent way? Did the men who signed up truly understand what they were condemning future generations to suffer? I know little of Nicholas Cavendish, who's coming of age was the catalyst for my torment, but what I've seen and heard from his wife, suggests he really is trying to change the future for generations to come. Will it be possible in a society where there is such deep-rooted malevolence, and where there are members who still believe they have a right to behave as their forebears did? Theft, abuse, lies, it's all second nature to the generation my father belongs to. Can our generation, Nicholas, Victoria, Theo, William, Tamara, and I really change it, or is it a dream which will end in defeat and stricter rules for the future to prevent an insurgency again?

I shift from the bed and wrap a dressing gown around myself, despite the warmth of the last few days, there is a chill in the air this morning. Perhaps it's the first frosts on the way, or a sign of impending doom bearing down upon us at a frantic pace. I can only pray for the first option.

My breath hitches when I notice the gun beside my bed. Theo must have left it there for me to protect myself, I don't even want to question how he came to have it because I know it must be illegal. The thought chills me to the bone that in order to ensure my safety when alone in this house where I'm supposed to be mistress I need a weapon capable of bringing death. It's not right. I open the drawer and put the gun inside. I won't be scared in my own home. I need to find the strength within me to help Theo end this.

I pick a change of clothes out of my wardrobe and head into the bathroom. A quick shower refreshes my senses, and I'm feeling a lot more relaxed than before. It's a new day, and a new start. Everything will be all right.

With a yawn and an exaggerated stretch of my arms, I blow away the final cobwebs of sleep and head downstairs for breakfast. The house is quiet. It's normally a hive of activity with staff milling around doing jobs to make sure everything runs properly. I was brought up believing a woman's place was to run the household. I'll have to speak to Theo about taking on some of the responsibility. I call for his butler, but nobody comes. An eerie feeling passes over me. This is not normal. Maybe Theo had his butler travel with him to see Victoria? No, he would've had him stay here to protect me. I tentatively push the door open to the dining room and am greeted by the horror of Theo's butler lying unmoving on the floor with a bullet hole in the centre of his forehead.

"Did you really think you'd get away with pulling a stunt like that against your own father?" The deep voice from behind me chills me to the bone.

"It wasn't a stunt." I turn and drop to my knees. The words leave my mouth when I know I should be silent. "I had to give Theo something, and it was the only thing I could think of."

Viscount Hamilton steps forward with several men flanking him on either side. I recognize the majority of them. They are members of the society. Men who were there the night I was purchased. He pulls me to my feet and pushes me hard against the wall.

"Lying little bitch." He whacks his hand hard across my

face. My ears ring with the force of it, and my head spins. "Your father came to me, barely alive. He was one of my biggest allies, but after my son did a number on him, he was questioning whether this is all worth it. I couldn't have that." The Viscount's lip curls up at the corners in a demonic smile. "Well, Lady Hamilton, now Countess of Linton, I hope you're happy? You caused the death of your father."

I try to feel guilt at the death of the man who was supposed to love and protect me, but I can't. He gave me away to a monster for money, and I'm unable to grieve for him. All I can do is wish him a speedy passage into hell. Another punch comes to my face, and my legs struggle to hold up my failing body.

"You've spoiled my son. He was supposed to be strong and a great leader, but you've made him weak. He wasn't supposed to take the photo to Nicholas. He was supposed to lead a riot against the Oakfield Society's current leaders with it. Get them sent to prison where I could finish them off. But no, you made him into a fool. Why would I want Victoria back? She's shown her true colors. I can't believe she succeeded in becoming the Duchess and making Nicholas a wimp at the same time. The women around me are conniving little bitches. They'll all get theirs though. A Duchess will fetch a good price."

The laugh that comes from the Viscount scares me more than the thought of being raped by him again. I can deal with that. I can shut my mind away from his torment because I know he's the one who is inadequate and wrong, not me. But to hear him talk of his own daughter in a way that describes her downfall brings bile to my throat. The ends of my hair are pulled hard, and I'm dragged across the room and thrown to one of the men who accompanied the Viscount.

"Take her to the car. She'll fetch a good price as well."

I'm handed over to the other man, and he wraps his arms around me, over my breasts, with his filthy digits digging into my flesh.

"Remember, Joanna, what happens now, you started. We end Nicholas and William Cavendish tonight. My daughter will be sold, and Theo...he dies. He's served his purpose and has now been misguided by his willful whore of a wife. I made an error marrying you to him. I thought him stronger than to fall for your sorrowful eyes and magical pussy, but I was mistaken." The Viscount sneers at me. He's talking about selling his own daughter and murdering his son. This man isn't human. He's a devil, walking the Earth. I can't take in what I'm hearing. The person holding me lowers one of his hands down to the cleft between my thighs.

"Can I sample this magical pussy while we wait?"

As he heads toward the stairs the Viscount replies.

"Do with it what you want. Don't break it though. That's my job."

The man who's haunted my nightmares since he bought me disappears, and I'm dragged out of the house and toward the back of a waiting car. I try my hardest to free myself. I can't believe this is happening again. I want the nightmare to end.

"Theo!" I scream, willing him to appear, but I know in my heart it's a miracle that won't happen. If I'm to stop this chain of events, I need to save myself.

The man holding me slaps his hand over my mouth to prevent me from screaming. I bite down into his flesh until I taste blood, and he yelps in pain.

"Fucking bitch." He throws me onto the ground and sends a kick into my stomach. I curl instantly up into a ball and groan as an explosion of agony cascades through my body. *Think Joanna,* I tell myself. *You need to be sensible and strong.*

The man kicks me again, this time in my head. I see stars, and the pain in my body is bordering on the limit of what I can cope with. He lowers himself to the ground before flipping me over, so I'm on all fours, and pulling me back against his hard length.

"I was going to let you have it in the softness of the car, but I think a gravel driveway is better for you." He lifts the skirt up I'm wearing and fumbles to remove my underwear. *Strength Joanna, strength.* He leans over me, and I sense an opportunity. Throwing my head back, I connect with his face. I hear his nose crunch, and he loosens his grip and falls to the gravel. I may have just killed him, but I've no time to think about that. My entire body hurts, and I need to get away. Thinking quickly, I search around in his pockets for the car keys. Finding them, I rush to the car and start the engine just as one of the other men comes out and sees what's happening. I don't have time to think. I've not driven in so long, but it all comes back to me, thankfully. I push my foot down on the accelerator and speed down the driveway. The second man rushes at the car in an attempt to stop me. I don't stop, though, not even when he goes flying over the bonnet. I speed out of the driveway and onto the road.

Think Joanna...Police? I need to go to them. No, I can't. I have to warn Theo and Victoria. I have to get to Oakfield Hall. I've only been there once, but I remember the journey and how to get there. Trying not to draw attention to myself, I keep my driving as normal as possible. There must be a large dent in the bonnet of the car where I hit the man, so I drive sensibly. It's still early, but the roads are starting to get busy with yet another commuter rush hour. I take a few wrong turns on the way with my hands shaking violently on the wheel, and my eyes flicking into the rear-view mirror every few seconds to make sure I'm not being followed. I don't know how long it takes me to make the journey, but eventually I make it to the Cavendish's house and slam to a halt in the middle of their driveway. Nicholas appears at the front door with William behind him. Both have a look of concern on their face. As I get out of the car, all the adrenaline I've been feeling dissipates, and I fall to the ground as my tears start to fall.

"Theo!" I shout at them as they both run to my side. Nicholas picks me up and carries me into the house while William calls for hot water, brandy, and bandages.

"Joanna, what happened?"

"Where's Theo?" I ask again.

"He's gone to the police with Victoria and Tamara?"

"No." I break down in heaving sobs again. "You have to find him."

William hands me the brandy brought in by the butler, and Nicholas moves back to allow a maid to step up and start cleaning my wounds.

"Speak slower. What happened?" Nicholas questions.

"You have to go after them. The Viscount came for me. He's going to end this today. He's going to destroy you and William, sell Victoria and Tamara, and kill Theo. Please, you have to save him. Save everyone. I want this to end."

CHAPTER NINETEEN

THEODORE

The car is silent for most of the journey. All of us are lost deep in our own thoughts. I'm struggling, and I'm not afraid to admit it. The man I grew up worshipping as my father is nothing but a fraud and a liar. I don't know for certain if it was my father who hurt Joanna. I've not heard it directly from her lips, but my heart already tells me it was. I don't know how I can ever make it up to her or rid her of the pain she must be feeling. Does she even really want me as a husband? A constant reminder of the man who abused her. I can't think about that, now. As we draw nearer to the police station, Victoria nestles in closer to my side. Tamara rubs at her stomach.

"How are you feeling?" I nod at where her hand rests upon the baby growing inside her.

"Is it that obvious? I'd be fine it it wasn't for William fussing over me all the time." She rolls her eyes.

"William is a little over protective of her at the moment," Victoria adds. "You'd think she's made of glass and could break at any moment."

"He's a good man. He's just looking after you." We all become silent again at my words. "So's Nicholas." I kiss the top of my sister's head. "I'm glad you both found the two of them."

"We wish it were under other circumstances, but I wouldn't be without Nicholas," Victoria responds.

"Nor I without William," Tamara adds.

I reach out for my other sister, how strange that sounds, and squeeze her hand.

"I'm just glad you're both married, and I don't have to worry about the two of you out partying together."

"Protective big brother," Victoria teases, but the smile on Tamara's face is what I really notice. She's gone from having no family to being in a loving relationship with her husband and the middle child in a sibling sandwich between me and Victoria.

"Don't you know it, sisters," I reply before turning to look out the window as the streets of London flash past. I look back at Tamara. "I'm really sorry about your mother. She was a special person in our household. I'll miss her."

Tears pool in Tamara's eyes, mourning the loss of a woman who, I now know, had to deal with so much but came out the other side still fighting for her daughter.

"She's at peace, and I'm going to continue her legacy. Victoria is as well."

"Yes, we are." Victoria smiles at her best friend and sister. "Nicholas is changing the society. We're going to be looking to do more philanthropic work. Nicholas is in the process of setting up the Elsie Bennett fund to provide grants for children to study art."

"That sounds a fantastic idea," I reply with enthusiasm. It's something I've always been interested in doing but have been hampered by my need to learn how to be a Viscount. A title, which I've found out today, I've been the holder of for a few months. It's just another thing to take in. I wonder where it's all going to end?

The car suddenly screeches to a halt, and we all jerk forward in our seatbelts. I manage to stop myself from banging my head on the seat in front of me, but Victoria isn't so lucky and rubs her head in a daze. Leaning forward, Tamara begins to open the partition between our compartment and the driver's. Suddenly, a blood curdling scream comes from her, telling me something is seriously wrong.

"Run!" she shouts as she frantically tries to undo her seat belt, but her hands are fumbling against the release button. I undo mine and set her and Victoria both free. We jump out of the car, but before we can run anywhere, guns are pointed directly at our heads.

"You had to allow your cock to do the thinking, didn't you, son?" My father gets out of one of the vehicles surrounding our own. A bullet hole has broken the glass of our windshield, and behind the shattered mess is the bloodied face of our driver. Now I know what Tamara was screaming at.

"What is going on, Father?" I decide to try and play dumb until I can formulate a better plan. My father is obviously a dangerous and volatile man. To hold up a car in daylight with people around is a sign of desperation, and a last resort.

"Don't play dumb. I know the little whore of yours has told you everything."

"What?" I screw my face up trying to feign confusion. "I've just collected Victoria and Tamara from Nicholas. I've got them back. He's taken Rose somewhere, but I'm working on that."

Victoria must catch on to what I'm doing.

"Please, Father. He has my daughter. I don't know where he took her. You have to find her. He'll hurt her I know it."

My father hesitates for a minute, his eyes narrowing as he tries to make sense of the scene unfolding before him. I can see the questions as to the validity of it running through his head.

He motions with a wave of his hand and his men step up to us and search us. My phone is removed from my pocket. Victoria's and Tamara's are taken as well. They are handed to my father who drops them onto the ground before smashing them with his feet. Victoria and Tamara both scream.

"What was that for?" I protest.

"First lesson, Theo. Nicholas doesn't give up anything easily. He'll have them tracked."

I lower my head to show deference to his superiority and acknowledge my mistake.

"I'm sorry, Father. I was just so glad to get them away from him. Joanna has told me things about what he's done to her. I couldn't bear to think of him hurting my sister in that way."

"No." My father steps forward toward Victoria. I can see her hands shaking as she struggles to maintain her composure and keep up the web of lies we're weaving. I hadn't thought about it until now, but this must be one of the first times she's seen our father since he gave her away. I've always visited her alone because she never wanted to see him. Why didn't I question everything sooner? I've been so blinded by the affection I have for this man who doesn't deserve it.

"Did he hurt you badly, my little one?" He strokes his hand down Victoria's face, and she lets out an anguished cry.

"He was horrible, Daddy," she whimpers, and he pulls her into his arms. "Shush, my darling girl. It'll be better now. You'll never have to see him again."

"Thank you." Her voice cracks as she replies.

Next, he turns to Tamara.

"And you?"

My father steps toward Tamara, and I say a silent prayer for her to continue our charade until I can figure out a better way to get us to safety. Someone must have heard the gunshot and reported it. Police must be on the way. We just need to buy more time.

"They spin lies and draw you in to the point where you don't know what the truth is anymore." Her voice is almost robotic, but the tears trickling down her cheeks tell of the emotions crashing through her body.

"Lies. You've been surrounded by lies all your life, haven't you?" My father is in front of Tamara, now, and he reaches out to touch her cheek.

"Far too many."

"Hmmm." My father hums as he strokes down Tamara's cheek and across her shoulder bone. "Lies about your birth, lies about your friends, and lies about your mother." The last word is said with such malevolence it freezes even my own blood. It has the opposite effect on Tamara though. It ignites her blood into a fiery tirade directed at our father.

"You bastard, don't you dare mention my mother. I know

what you did. I know just who you are." She brings her fist up and aims it at him, but he catches it and twists her around, so she's pulled close against him. "It's time for Daddy to take what's his," he says as he leers at her, and I realize for the first time the true level of his depravity. When Joanna told me William called her Tamara, it's now obvious to me that it wasn't William who said it but my father.

"No." Victoria reacts before I can. She lunges for her friend and sister but is pulled back by one of my father's men. She punches and kicks out at him until he knocks her over the head with a gun, and she falls as if lifeless into his arms.

"Get them in the car," my father orders. I try to step forward, but I am prevented from doing so by a gun raised in my face and two men pulling me back. My strength can't match their numbers. The man holding Victoria drags her to the car. Tamara is handed over to another man and is hauled screaming toward the same vehicle. They are pushed into the backseat, and it speeds away.

My father steps toward me.

"Such a disappointment. You could have ruled at my side, but I won't have the weak with me. I'll be the King of Oakfield by the end of the day, and you..." He looks at the man pointing the gun at my temple. "...will be dead. You shouldn't have fallen for the whore. Mind you, her pussy is wonderful. I'm the one who took her first, and I'll continue to take her for as long as I allow her to live."

Despite being held at gunpoint, I lunge for my father but never make it. The men surrounding him stop me and throw me to the ground. A hail of fists thump into my body and face as I watch my father get into a vehicle and depart in a screech of tires. He's won. I've lost my sisters and possibly my wife if my father's words mean he's also taken her. I should've listened sooner.

Everyone steps back, and the man who originally held the gun to my head then steps forward. He points it down at me, and I know this is the end of my life. I've failed in my pledge to my wife. More car tires screech, and the man pointing the gun at my head suddenly flies into the air and lands with a thud on the ground. His body twisted and broken. The two men remaining, set upon the new vehicle, and I see Nicholas and William emerge from it. Both have weapons drawn and make quick work of disposing of the two men. Nicholas throws his phone to William,

"Call Matthew Carter and get him to send in a clean-up squad."

William nods and flips open the phone.

"Where are Victoria and Tamara?" He looks past me at the car.

"My father took them, a few minutes ago. They went that way," I respond indicating the direction I saw the vehicles take.

Nicholas curses but still helps me to my feet. I lean forward and cough up a little blood from the beating.

"Get Matthew to trace Victoria," Nicholas orders William

"He broke their phones," I inform him.

"My wife is a walking tracker. Do you think I'd let something so precious be left vulnerable? Don't worry. I'll have a location for her in a few minutes, and we'll go and get her. Let's get back to the house and clean you up. There's someone waiting to see you there."

"Who?" Nicholas helps me into his car as several other cars sweep into the section of the road we've just committed chaos in. The occupants of the vehicles emerge and eagerly set about cleaning up. This is all alien to me, and it feels like I've suddenly become embroiled in a James Bond film.

"Your wife." Nicholas smiles at me. "She escaped your father and probably saved your life."

"What?" I stumble into the car, and we drive back to Oakfield Hall with me sitting in a daze of disbelief. My wife survived—we have a chance. We just need to save my sisters to get our happy ending.

CHAPTER TWENTY

JOANNA

I don't think I've ever begged time to go so quickly. I just want to know what's happening as I pace up and down the living room of Oakfield Hall. My hands are shaking, and I keep humming to myself to settle my nerves.

The soft murmurs of a waking baby in the bassinet beside me draw my attention. Nicholas left in such a hurry he entrusted the care of his daughter to me while supervised by a stern looking butler at all times. Apparently, it's the nanny's day off, but she's making her way back from visiting her cousin in Oxford as a matter of urgency.

Little Rose coos after her sleep before getting a bit more

disgruntled when her mother doesn't appear. I look at the butler, and his eyes widen in fear of the tiny human in the crib.

"What's wrong with her ladyship?" he asks, and I try to stifle my amusement that a young baby is being formally referred to as 'her ladyship'.

"I suspect she needs changing and feeding." I go over to the cot and dangle my hand in. I've taken a quick shower after my assault and wrapped myself up in one of Victoria's dressing gowns, so I'm clean. Little Rose looks up at me with a squint, trying to focus. Her crying becomes a little more panicked when she realizes I'm not her mother or father.

"It's all right, little lady." I bring her up into my arms and rock her gently. "Daddy has just gone to get your mummy and Uncle Theo. They'll be back soon." I pat under her bottom to feel her diaper, and it feels full.

"Is that uncomfortable? Let's get you changed while Mr. Alfred arranges for your bottle to be brought up." Before she left, I was told Victoria requested some milk for Rose. Alfred quickly disappears to retrieve it, and I'm left with a grumpy baby. I carry her over to the changing table and quickly make her more comfortable. We then settle down in a chair and wait for the milk. I can't help but fall instantly in love with her. A perfect angel born into a world of chaos. I can only hope she'll have a better future than the one her mother and I have experienced.

The door to the nursery opens and a tired looking Nicholas walks in with a bottle. I stand and hand him his daughter. He looks like he needs her.

"What happened?" I'm too afraid to ask, but I know I must.

"The Viscount has taken Victoria and Tamara. We saved Theo, though." A noise behind the Duke distracts my attention, and I see my husband leaning against William. He's been wounded.

"Theo." I run to him and fling my arms around him. I'm trying my hardest not to cry, but an anguished sob leaves my throat.

"It's ok. I'm all right." He kisses the top of my head. "You did so well escaping and getting here. I'm so proud of you."

"I'm sorry," I whimper into his chest.

"I know the truth now. We can put a stop to this," Theo reassures me. I feel the room close in with the tension, and the three men surrounding me look urgently down at the phone in William's hand.

"What is happening with Victoria and Tamara? Have you called the police?"

"No," Nicholas replies curtly.

"We'll deal with it our way," William adds, and I don't dare ask what he means even though in my heart I already know, and it won't be pretty.

The mobile in William's hand rings, and we all freeze and stare at it for a few seconds before he answers and puts it on speaker.

"William Cavendish."

"It's Carter."

"You got them?" The conversation is clipped and straight to the point.

"We've got an issue with the tracker. Hamilton must have his own people with links to MI5. Only they could block the signal ." The dominant voice from the other side of the phone explains.

William looks at his brother. Nicholas comes closer and asks,

"What are you doing about it?"

"Everything I can. I wanted to give you a quick update. Ryan and I are going to go and get some answers from the grid itself. You'll have to give me another hour, and then I'll have a location."

"I don't know if we have an hour." Nicholas cradles his daughter who's happily sucking on her bottle, unaware of the tension in the room.

"I'll have to bash heads together harder, then."

The phone goes dead.

"Who's that?" I question.

"A friend," Nicholas replies, not giving me anymore than I need to know. "I'm going to sit with my daughter. Fetch me when he phones back." The Duke turns away, effectively dismissing us from his presence. William directs us out of the room and down the hall to a spare bedroom.

"You can freshen up in here, Theo. There's a change of clothes in the wardrobe as well. I'll be downstairs in the study. I'm going to go through all the papers Tamara has on the Viscount. Hopefully there'll be something in them that can give us a clue to their location."

Theo nods at him, and says, "I wish I could give you more. We've already checked the one location I knew about. I'll keep thinking of others. We'll find them."

William doesn't say anything. He just flicks his ear and nose before marching off down the corridor while Theo leads me into the room.

"We should be doing something," I plead with him, but he shakes his head.

"Nicholas and William know what they're doing."

"But they are so calm, and with what he's capable of..." I falter on the last words. Does my husband truly understand what his father can be like?

"William and Nicholas are anything but calm, believe me. They are prepared to end this to save their wives. Don't mistake deadly intentions for calmness." Theo pulls his shirt off over his head, and I notice the bruising on his chest. He rubs a hand over it and looks at me.

"I'm starting to learn what my father is capable of. I think you need to tell me the rest."

My stomach drops. I knew this moment would come but the thought of reliving my nightmares in front of my husband scares me more than the actual abuse itself. I'm scared of losing him. What if he doesn't love me anymore as a result of what his father did to me? I slump down into a nearby chair

"Why didn't you tell me?" Theo shakes his head at me. "My own father!"

"I wanted to. I don't know if I can explain it. I was kept hidden for a year for a reason. He had to condition me, so I couldn't think for myself." I get up from the chair again, finding it really difficult to talk about what happened. I've been instructed not to say anything and accept I'm the Viscount's property to do with as he wants. I no longer have a right to a thought of my own, but I do have thoughts, I'm having them now, and it scares me so much.

"I have to try and explain this to you, don't I?" I say pacing the room.

"Yes," Theo replies despondently.

"When I was brought to the house, the same one we were married in, I was placed naked in a small basement room. I was left there for weeks with nobody to talk to. Food and water were thrown my way, but I wasn't addressed. I had to do all my business in a small bucket, which was occasionally emptied. I had nothing to read, and no concept of what night or day was. The only sounds around me were the noises of the building itself. Do you know how noisy an old house can be? It's deafening at times." I stop pacing by a window and stare out at the green pastures below. "Eventually your father started to visit me. He didn't speak to me. He'd just stand there at the door staring at me. This went on for another couple of weeks. Everything was starting to blur by then. It could have been days, but to me, it felt like weeks. I was starved of the sound of humanity...starved of the sound of a voice no matter what it said. I would have begged to be called a whore if it meant I heard something other than the creaks of the house. One day, he did talk to me, and it was like a choir of angels rejoicing hallelujah. Do you know what he said?"

I shift position, so I can see Theo's face. His breathing is even, but I can tell he's trying to control his emotions. His fists are tightly clenched, and there is a tic in his jaw.

"I don't."

"On your knees." I lower myself down to kneel before my husband. "I couldn't believe what I was hearing. I was stunned. I just stood there, so he shut the door and disappeared. He didn't come the next day, or the day after that. I craved for him to return. How sick is that?" I allow my hands to fall at my sides and hang loosely while bowing my head, so I'm looking down at the floor. "He came back after three days and said the same three words, 'on your knees.' This time, I obeyed. He'd won and broken me. Over the next few weeks, months, I don't know how long, the same treatment was repeated. If I didn't do something he wanted, I would be left alone in the darkness until he reappeared, and I obeyed. The first time he wanted me to give oral, I didn't hide my teeth enough, and he thought I was going to bite him. I was beaten black and blue and left alone for so long. I thought I'd been abandoned, and left to die. Food was minimal during that time, and I rationed the portions I was given. I remember when he returned I was so grateful to see him, especially as he brought me a small bar of chocolate. It's stupid." I can't stop the tears. I'm sobbing now, but they are freeing and needed. "I allowed him to come down my throat three times that day. I swallowed every bit of him and was rewarded with a speech of how I was a dirty little whore, and that the next time he came to see me, he would be taking my pussy over and over again. I should have hated what he said to me, but I didn't. I wanted more. I wanted him to call me every degrading name in the world. I didn't care because at least someone was talking to me."

It's Theo's turn to get up, this time. I don't look up from my bowed position. I just listen to the sound of his feet as they march to the bedroom door before hearing him furiously pull the door open, and then slam it shut behind him as he leaves.

I let out an anguished cry and collapse down into a ball on the floor. I knew he would hate me. I'm disgusting. How can anyone crave the sort of abuse I did? A loud masculine roar comes from the hallway, and I shrink further into myself. A deafening thud pounds into the wall, not once but twice, and is followed by smashing glass.

"I'll kill him," Theo yells, and there are more sounds of breaking glass.

"Enough." There is another deep voice, and I recognize it as Nicholas'. "Save the anger for when we find him. Between the three of us, we'll tear him apart limb from limb."

The hallway goes silent for a few minutes, and then the door opens again, and Theo re-enters the room. He comes straight to me, and sweeping me up into his arms, he carries me to the bed where he brings my face up to meet his.

"You'll never bow before anyone again. You'll stand proudly upright as a strong woman. I'll fill our entire house with noise. It will never be silent again. I'm sorry…I'm so sorry I didn't realize the truth sooner. I'm just glad he arranged for us to marry, so I was able to get you away from him for a while."

I can't stop the whimper on my breath.

"No." Theo shakes his head. "Please tell me he didn't."

"I wish I could. He came to me the night after we first made love. It was him who gave me the photo and demanded I give it to you. He's been playing games from the start. He told me I had to get pregnant with your child."

Theo pushes away from me in disgust.

"That's why you pleaded with me to take you on our wedding night."

"I was so scared. He told me what would happen to me would be worse if I didn't do it. Then he started threatening your life. I'm scared of him, Theo. He's a monster, and I don't know how to get out from under his shadow. Even now if he walked into this room, I'd fall to my knees and let him do to me what he wants. I don't know how to say no."

Theo places his head in his hands. When he looks back up at me, I can see tears in his eyes.

"Don't you see. You've already saved yourself. You did get away from him. You came here. That was you beating his rule. His spell on you is broken."

He comes back to me and kisses my lips passionately and then places his hand over my heart.

"This is what gave you the strength to beat him. Love…our love. You are free, Joanna. You've just got to start believing it yourself. There is no more silence in the world. Even if it's quiet, you'll hear the sound of the beating of your heart entwined with mine."

"I'm free." The concept is alien to me. I test it on my lips and like it. "I can be your wife?"

He nods.

"Yes, but only after you learn to be yourself."

"I thought you'd hate me."

"Never." Theo pulls me into his arms, and we settle back against the bed. My eyelids grow heavy with the exhaustion of telling him everything. Theo continues, "No, the person I hate is my father. He's gotten away with too much for too long now. As soon as we find out where he is, we're putting a stop to this. His reign of terror is over. It's about time he learned the correct way to treat a woman."

CHAPTER TWENTY-ONE

THEODORE

*J*oanna and I rest for no longer than half an hour before the need to find my sisters gets the better of both of us. We make our way down to the office where William is surrounded by papers, which he's frantically searching through for any evidence of where my father could be hiding. Nicholas follows us down with a baby monitor in his hand and immediately picks up a pile of his own papers. He looks exhausted, and I can see the love both men have for my sisters. They may be quiet and tired of waiting, but they'll be vicious when it comes to the rescue. A mobile sits next to William within easy access for when the call we're all longing for comes through. In total, the girls have been missing for an hour, and it's been the longest hour of all our lives. I know what my father is truly capable of, now. I would like to think his paternal nature would kick in and protect Tamara and Victoria, but after hearing the way he treated Joanna and ordered my execution, I know he's incapable of compassion.

"I'm going to see if the chef can get us all a sandwich and a drink." Joanna stands up on tiptoes and kisses my lips. "We need to keep our energy up."

Nicholas looks up from his papers and signals it's a good idea before asking, "Would you mind checking on Rose as well? She's sleeping but is unsettled. I think she knows her mummy is missing. A feminine touch might help."

"Of course." Joanna lets go of my hand and leaves the room, shutting the door behind her.

"How is she?" William looks up from where he's been studying a piece of paper that looks like a bank statement.

"Ok." I pick up a couple of the sheets he's yet to examine and start looking over them. "It's going to take a while, but she's strong."

We fall into silence for a short while. Each of us are lost in our own thoughts as we search for something, anything, to tell us where my father could be. The paper I have lists financial transactions from his bank. Different amounts relating to donations, household expenditures, and a couple of costs for properties he owns.

"Has someone checked our property in Yorkshire?"

"Yes," Nicholas replies. "It seems he moved Joanna's keeper, Camilla Fentress, up there. She's dead, killed by a bullet to the center of her forehead. He's obviously been cleaning house, getting ready to take over from me."

I remember the woman who was there when I was married

to Joanna. She seemed kind, but I know better now. I won't mourn her death. I hope she suffered.

"We've got to be missing something." William throws down his pile of papers. "I need to get Tamara back. She's pregnant, and Joanna warned Victoria about the Viscount and his fascination with her."

"He made Joanna dress up as Tamara," I blurt out.

"What?" William is on his feet and thumping his hands on the desk.

"She told me it was you, and you had a wig made like Tamara when she had long hair."

William and Nicholas look at each other.

"Fuck!" Nicholas exclaims. "He's sicker than I thought."

"What?" I question.

"Tamara was taken by an old associate of the society, a perverted man named Lord West. We were late rescuing her, and the Viscount got there first. I didn't understand it at that point, but I do now," William explains.

"Sorry you've lost me?"

"While she was kidnapped, Tamara's hair had been chopped short, but we never found the hair that was removed. We assumed it had been thrown on the fire, but I've now got a feeling perhaps it was taken by the Viscount." William goes over to the corner of the room and pours a glass of what looks like brandy. He waves the decanter at me, and I nod to say yes.

"Perhaps what he did to Tamara's mother twisted his mind. I wonder if it was the first time he'd raped a woman?" Nicholas joins us, and William pours him a glass.

"First time?" These two brothers know so much more of what is happening around me than I do. I've been kept in the dark and am catching up quickly.

"When he raped Elsie and conceived Tamara," William

informs me, and we all remain silent for a moment and take a sip of drink.

"I can't help but think it was more. Possibly a result of the trials and what his parents put him through. If it wasn't for Victoria, I'm not sure my mind would have survived what our father ordered me to do." Nicholas muses into the bottom of his glass.

"I don't understand how they've been able to get away with treating women the way they have for so long. When my father bought Joanna, he just assumed the marriage between me and her would take place." Nicholas shrugs at me. "And it was never suggested I should be allowed to choose my own bride. Have generations of our families been so warped that they haven't been able to see right from wrong?"

"Eight generations," William mulls into his brandy glass.

"How many women have suffered at their hands?" I query and take another mouthful of the amber nectar.

"That we know of? Over the centuries, the sum total of the chosen ladies given to a Duke on his thirtieth birthday is… forty-three." Nicholas answers before shutting his eyes as the pain of the number sinks in with William and me.

"You know?" The younger Cavendish is shocked at his brother's answer.

"I went through all the papers shortly after I took over as the Duke. I learned the name of every single girl. Our mother,"—he looks at William and then at me—"your mother. They are both on the list. Nearly all died young. Your mother, Joanna and Victoria are the only survivors."

"My mother was one?" I can't believe what I'm hearing. I know my parents have never been a romantic couple, but it makes sense now why she's never really been around. She escaped as soon as she could, and my father was too busy tormenting other women to care. "Tradition was followed in my father's case and in mine. A rejected girl bought to marry?"

"Yes, every Hamilton is descended from one of the girls since the inception of the society." Nicholas shakes his head at me.

I stand there dumbfounded at what I'm hearing.

"I can't get my head around this. How have they got away with it for so long?"

"By having the right people in their pockets. People who'll turn a blind eye to what has been happening. Judges, police, senior politicians, even members of the royal family in the past. The aristocracy has been rotten for years, but I won't let it be that way for Rose." Nicholas slams his now empty glass down onto table in a defiant response.

"Too much sex of the wrong kind, if you ask me," William adds, and that earns a chuckle from Nicholas. "Small dicks with no ability to please a woman properly."

"You always have a way of putting things, brother, that lightens the mood." Nicholas slaps his brother on the back.

"I'm just saying it takes a real man to treat a woman properly and earn her respect. You don't get that by abusing her or ordering her around like a dog. You worship her and love her with as much affection as you can give even though men are shit at stuff like that, and they'll make mistakes. Or as in my case where their brain doesn't work the same as everyone else's, and they'll end up telling their wife she doesn't look good in the new dress she's just bought." William smirks

"Some women will say that's a good thing," Nicholas points out, and I nod in agreement.

"Not when you say she looks like the bride of Frankenstein, because the outfit was far too black for my liking." William screws his face up and then finishes his brandy.

"You didn't," I gasp.

"She thought I meant her hair and make-up as well as the dress. It was an honest mistake. I make them often. She should know by now."

"She does. Don't worry." Nicholas slaps his brother on the back again, and we all go quiet, hoping Tamara will get a chance to spend more time being told the honest truth about her outfits by her husband.

"I'm sorry I doubted you two." I finally break the silence. "I can see you both adore my sisters. I'm glad they have you. What you're trying to do for the society is going to help so many people. It will help to right the wrongs of the past."

"It will." Nicholas pushes away from where we are congregated and goes over to a safe in the wall. He punches in a code, which I don't see, and pulls out an old parchment.

"Is that what I think it is?" William cocks his head.

"The original society deeds. I think it's about time we wrote a new one."

Nicholas places the aging paper down and scribbles through the middle of it with the words, 'Null and Void.' He then turns it over and starts writing.

It is hereby claimed on the eighth day of the eleven month of the year twenty nineteen that a new charter for the society of Oakfield is to be adopted. From this point forth, all violence against women will result in summary expulsion from the society. The purpose for the society will now be to educate future generations of women who wish to learn the creative arts such as painting, literature, drama, and music. We will all work together to ensure they have the necessary skills to help them find their own way in life. Past wrongs will be righted. Hope is our new motto.

Underneath, he signs his name, Nicholas Cavendish, Duke of Oakfield, with a flourish and hands the pen to William, who signs as the Earl of Lullington. William hands me the pen, and I look at him.

"You were born a part of this, remember. Together, we are the ones who can change it."

I take the pen and sign my name, Viscount Theodore Hamilton, Earl of Linton.

A soft clapping comes from behind us, and we turn to see Joanna standing there with a big smile on her face.

"I love the idea. I hope I'm going to be allowed to help." She comes over to us and stands at my side. I look down at the pen, then back to her, and then to Nicholas. He nods. I look to William, and he does the same.

"Woman are now a part of the society and not in the way they were before." I hand her the pen, and she looks at me confused.

"I don't understand?"

"Sign it."

"But?"

"Sign it," Both William and Nicholas tell her at the same time.

"There are no more unequals in this society. We are all one."

Joanna takes the pen from me, and next to my name she signs, Lady Joanna Hamilton, Countess of Linton, and then places the pen down.

"Now we just need to bring the Duchess of Oakfield and Countess of Lullington home to sign it as well."

At the same time, we all turn our heads to the mobile phone sitting on William's desk. It must hear our silent prayers because it starts to ring.

CHAPTER TWENTY-TWO

JOANNA

"They're at Seven, Winchester Place. My men are on the way. See you there."

The phone goes dead, and I watch Theo as he stumbles backward and down into a chair. He knows the address—I'm certain of it.

"Theo?" I stroke his shoulder while Nicholas and William retrieve guns and other weapons from within a locked cupboard. "What is it?"

"My mother."

He's gone as white as a sheet and pulls his phone out of his pocket. Nicholas grabs it off him before he has a chance to call anyone. The elder Cavendish brother drops the phone onto the floor and stamps on it with his foot. "Don't be stupid."

"Hey." Theo scrambles to pick up the pieces of his broken mobile. "I need to warn her."

"They've been there for over an hour now. It'll be too late." Nicholas hands Theo a gun. "The society girls all die young. Let's hope your mother is the last one, and we can save my wife and your sister before it's too late."

I'm looking between the two men, wondering what's going on. What has Theo's mother got to do with this? William appears at my side and hands me a gun. I look down at it and back up at him as if to say 'what am I supposed to do with this?'

"Seven, Winchester Place, is just down the road. It's where Theo and Victoria's mother lives...lived. We've got to hope he sent her away rather than the alternative." He nods at the gun in my hand. "You know how to use it?"

"Yes," I say, stunned. The Viscount has spoken to me a few times about his wife, Lady Celia, during my time in his captivity. I know she was one of the ladies who was given to Nicholas' father. She wasn't chosen and was sold to the Viscount's father. Apparently, they were instantly married that night. She never had to experience the year of being hidden away and tortured like I did. No, she was taken the first night and conceived Theo. I remember the Viscount telling me about how he planned Victoria's birth to ensure she was one of the chosen for the next generation. She was nearly not born. The Countess had fallen pregnant with another child, originally, but an early test showed it to be a boy. She was forced to have an abortion, and then the Viscount had spent all his time 'fucking her hard', his words not mine, to ensure she conceived a girl. He took great delight in being rewarded with

Victoria a month before the cut-off. His wife's job done, he set her up in her own house, so he could continue with his business of being a Viscount and raising his daughter to be as virtuous as possible, ready for her debut into the society. He told me he hated his wife. She was weak and cried for her lost son all the time. She'd found out about Tamara as well and had berated him so much he'd been forced to break her jaw, so she'd shut up until it was fixed. Prior to him taking me, I don't think he'd seen her in years. He'd told Theo and Victoria she'd met another man, and she'd limited her contact with them. This will be another story I'll have to tell my husband—another truth I'll have to deliver to him, which will break even more of his spirit. He looks a defeated man at the moment, standing there looking at his gun as if he'd rather point it at his own head than anyone else's.

William breaks me out of my thoughts by handing me spare rounds and a bulletproof vest.

"What are you doing?" Theo steps forward and grabs the vest.

"Making sure she's safe during the assault." William looks at Theo as though it's obvious what he's doing. It is really, but I can see my husband has other ideas.

"She's not coming with us. She can help look after Rose along with your nanny now she's returned." Theo takes the gun from me, and I stand there compliant. It's still my nature not to argue. I think that will take a long time to recover from.

"We don't have time for this." Nicholas, who has finished preparing, sticks his head out the door to the office and calls for his car to be readied, "Let's go."

William places his hand on the document we've all just signed and points out the signatures. "All for one, Theo. She needs this more than we do. She needs closure. Don't stop her from getting it." The younger brother goes to stand with his sibling, and they both look impatiently back at us to make a decision.

"Do you want to go?" Theo asks me.

I hesitate over an answer. I want to see the Viscount die. I'd love to be the one to kill him, but what if I get in the way or get captured again? I realize I'm scared, but that's only natural. There's a bigger picture here than my fear: Tamara and Victoria. They need to be rescued, and my joining them may be the distraction needed.

"Yes," I respond to Theo and hold my hand out for the weapon and vest. He sighs heavily but hands them back to me.

"Stay close to me."

"I will." We follow the Cavendish brothers out of the house and into a Range Rover. Nicholas drives, and his foot is instantly put to the floor, and we speed out of his estate and onto the roads of the suburbs of London. It's almost lunchtime now, but it seems like so much more time has passed since I woke this morning and found Viscount Hamilton in the house and Theo's butler dead. God, I haven't even told him about that yet. Turning, I squeeze his hand, and he looks down at me, his brows furrowed in concentration.

"Your butler is dead."

"I know. A clean-up crew has been to the house. He was a good man. I'll make sure he gets all the honors he deserves."

"Good."

We all fall silent again and contemplate the possible outcomes of the next few hours. Eventually several other vehicles join us. I don't need to ask, but I know these are the men who work for the mysterious Matthew Carter. I hope they are as well trained as those of the Viscount. I think we're going to need it. I try my hardest to think of the men around the Viscount. I've been with them, and I've seen them all. I could be of help here but remembering them means remembering my time with him. Sitting next to Theo, knowing we're heading to save Tamara and Victoria from the same fate, helps me conquer my fears, though.

"I remember him normally having two other men he kept with him all the time." William turns around from the front seat to look at me.

"Go on," he encourages, and Theo, who's sitting next to me, squeezes my hand.

"They aren't all properly trained, not the men closest to him, anyway. I think they are society men." I bite my lip. "One of them was old, very old. He has other people, ones he calls dispensable for better protection. They'll probably be outside. I remember seeing them from my window when I was transferred to a proper bedroom." I look to Theo. "After about nine months, he decided my training was complete, and he trusted me enough to move me out of the basement because I wasn't a flight risk. It's true, I wasn't. By that point, I didn't remember a life before being beholden to the Viscount. I do now, and I want it back."

"Do you remember the names of any of the men he kept close?" Nicholas asks while keeping his eyes on the road.

I shake my head and swallow down the rising bile. I don't know the names of any of the men. I blocked out what they called each other. I had to after they gang raped me.

"I'm sorry. I..." My voice breaks.

"It's ok." Theo brings my hand up to his lips and kisses it. "We'll make them all pay."

"I'm sorry to ask you, Joanna, but is there anything else you remember? Anything that could be helpful regarding the way he works."

I take a deep breath and try to think, but only one thing comes to mind.

"I think they'll be kept somewhere dark in the house... maybe a cellar if it has one. It's his way of disorientating you. He'll want Tamara and Victoria confused and scared. It's the way he breaks you."

William nods his thanks at me and pulling out his phone, he dials a number. It comes up on the Bluetooth in the car.

"Carter."

"Do you know the layout of the house?" William asks.

"It's in front of me. What do you need?"

"Does it have a basement or cellar?"

"Yes."

"That's where they are."

The cars stop outside a large country house in the middle of a busy area of London. It's surrounded on all sides by other properties. Two men stand guard outside. Within seconds, the people in the other car are out, and the two men are disarmed and secured. I'm shocked at the speed of it all. One of the men, a massively built man with a commanding look mixed with dreamy brown eyes, nods at Nicholas.

"Clear," he mouths, and we all get out of the car and follow behind the large man and three others. I'm surrounded by William and Theo. My gun is in my hand, and in my head, I'm running through all the things I need to do to ensure it works properly if I need to shoot it. The tension in the air is palpable. The door is kicked in, and two men standing in the hallway are shot with silenced guns. I pull my lips together tightly to stifle the scream threatening to escape. We need to be quiet.

"Please, let them be ok," I whisper a prayer to myself as we make our way through the house. We reach the kitchen via the entrance to the hall, and there, in the middle of the floor, lies a woman with blood pooling around her from a wound to the head. Her eyes are open but dead. I instantly grab hold of Theo's hand. I know who the woman is. His mother. A single tear tumbles down his cheek before he mouths.

"Let's end this. My father dies today."

CHAPTER TWENTY-THREE

THEODORE

I try my hardest not to look down at my mother. I know she's a person who for many years I've held hatred for because I thought she'd abandoned Victoria and me, but it was all lies. She was escaping the real villain in this story. I need him gone.

Matthew Carter presses a device against the door of the cellar and holds a finger up to silence us.

"Three men, two women," he relays back to us. "We need to go in quickly and hard. It's my guess the men will be armed. Two of them will make a grab for the women and use them as shields. They won't kill them, yet. They lose the bargaining chip if they do. Hamilton will no doubt have one of the ladies. Give me a few seconds, I want to try and ascertain their positions better."

We all nod in agreement with him, and he goes back to listening at the door. A few minutes later, his eyes go wide with fear, and he drops the listening device and pulls out his gun.

"We go in now. One of the women is about to be raped."

"Tamara," Joanna gasps from beside me, and Nicholas and I both step in front of William. I can physically see a change come about him. He's been calm and collected, up until this point, but his pupils darken to the point where I'm unable to see the color of his irises. He surges forward, but his brother and I hold him in place.

"Out of my way," William growls.

"Joanna sing hush little baby. Quickly, if he loses it when we go down there it could be the end of Victoria and Tamara," Nicholas orders as Matthew prepares his men, and they smash through the door into the cellar.

"Wh-What?" Joanna stutters in confusion.

"Do it!" Nicholas shouts.

> *"Hush, little baby, don't say a word,*
> *Mama's going to buy you a mocking bird.*
> *And if that mockingbird don't sing,*
> *Mama's going to buy you a diamond ring."*

Joanna sings, and William goes limp in our arms. His pupils shrink back, and his brown eyes reappear.

"I want my wife," he informs us, and both Nicholas and I step aside and allow him down into the cellar. I pull Joanna to my side and follow them down. The basement area is damp, and the smell of mold invades my nostrils. Is this similar to the place Joanna was hidden away? I turn back to her in the dim light of the stairway and can see the hesitance in her eyes, but then it's instantly masked with a determination so strong I can't help but feed from it.

We reach the bottom of the stairs and are faced with a stand-off. Matthew and his men are pointing guns at two men: one my father and another I recognize from visiting him. They each hold one of the women. My father stands behind Tamara, and the other man is behind Victoria who looks dazed and confused. A third man lies unmoving on the floor—blood has started to pool around him from a wound to his chest. I'm left in no doubt that he's dead or nearly there. It's a fatal wound, but I feel no sorrow for his death.

"You've changed your hair," William speaks first and cocks his head to where Tamara stands, wearing a wig of thick black hair.

"It wasn't my idea." She tries her hardest to struggle against my father's hold, but he's too strong for her, and there is a hesitancy in her movements, probably because of the child within her stomach.

Nicholas takes control of the situation with his commanding presence.

"It's over, Hamilton. Let the ladies go."

"It's not over until the blood in your body flows all over this floor," my father retorts and moves his gun from where it's pointed at Tamara's head and aims it straight toward Nicholas. He doesn't pull the trigger, though. He knows the speed of the men who have guns pointed at him is far superior to his own. He'd be dead before the bullet leaves the gun.

I push Joanna closer to William, and he tucks her behind him, so I can step forward to join his brother.

"It's over, Father. You've made too many mistakes. Put the gun down."

A lecherous sneer crosses his face.

"I see you've brought my little whore with you. I underestimated her ability to escape the way she did. I guess I'll have to work harder at breaking her when you're lying dead next to the Duke. So many titles for me to take. A whole new world to rule over."

"You sure it's only cigars he smokes and nothing a little stronger?" Matthew raises an eyebrow over at me.

"I'm beginning to wonder." I shrug my shoulders.

"Enough." My father steps forward with Tamara in front of him. His weapon is pointed at us, and we perform a dance around the room. He's working his way toward the door to escape. The trained men in our entourage try to prevent this, but there's little they can do with my sisters in the line of fire.

"We have to stop them," Joanna whispers behind me, and I look carefully over my shoulder to reassure her it'll be all right, but she's already moving forward to where my father stands. I instantly want to stop her, but Nicholas prevents me from moving.

"Give her a chance. She needs this."

Joanna walks between Nicholas and I and slowly lowers herself to her knees in front of my father. She bows her head, and a triumphant smirk crosses his face.

"Maybe I underestimated my skills, after all. Once a slave always a slave. Tamara and Victoria will make great pets for their new owners. Come here." All I can do is stand by and watch whatever Joanna's plan is unfold. She gets to her feet with her head still bowed and makes her way to stand next to him. At the same time, I see out the corner of my eye one of Matthew's men step closer to where the second man has Victoria. He's the weaker of the two and will be easier to take down. Nicholas slightly nods his head, and in the blink of an eye, the man holding Victoria is on the floor and dead with a bullet hole to his head, and she is free and in her husband's arms. With the distraction, Joanna pulls her weapon from where it was hidden in her thick jumper and points it at my father's head.

"Drop your gun," she orders. He doesn't move at first, but William and I descend on him with our own weapons drawn.

"It's over," I repeat. "Drop you weapon."

It seems like an age, but eventually my father accepts defeat and lowers his gun. He lets go of his hold on Tamara, and she runs to William while I take the weapon from my father.

"Why?" I ask him.

"Because I could," my father replies.

I shake my head and turn to give the weapon to one of the trained MI5 men in our group. My father uses my distraction and pushing past me, he tries to race up the stairs. He's not quick enough, though. A weapon fires, and the bullet goes straight into his leg, causing him to collapse down onto the ground. When I look down, there's smoke emerging from my own gun. It was me who shot him. Joanna comes quickly to my side while Nicholas and William leave Tamara and Victoria to drag my father back into the center of the room. He's screaming in pain. Nicholas removes the tie my father is wearing and stuffs it into his mouth to shut him up.

Matthew comes over and secures my father's hands with cuffs.

"I'll leave you six to finish this. We'll start cleaning upstairs. What do you want done about the woman?"

Nicholas looks at me, and Victoria lets out a cry.

"With Theo and Victoria's permission, I'd like to bury her with my mother and Tamara's. The three women who've given birth to the new generation of the society all together. While the three men: my father, Joanna's, and eventually the scum at my feet, who gave nothing but their sperm, will be forgotten for the evil deeds they committed."

"Please, Theo." Victoria begs as she slides down to sit on the floor. She looks exhausted and weak.

"Of course," I reply instantly and go to help support her. Joanna comes with me and sits down next to her.

"Is Rose ok?" Victoria asks immediately.

"She's fine. She has more guards around her than we have here." Joanna smiles weakly. She's exhausted as well.

While Matthew and the other men leave the six of us alone with my father, William and Tamara speak quietly in the corner of the room. Pulling the wig from her head, Tamara drops it onto the floor. Then William places his hand over her stomach, and she reassures him she's all right and wasn't hurt.

Nicholas stands over my father and addresses us, "I don't think I need to tell you what happens next. In order to put an end to this, I need to send a message. If you don't want to be involved, then you may leave with no questions asked. Victoria?"

She shakes her head. "I need closure."

"Tamara? William?"

"I want to see him suffer," Tamara announces through gritted teeth.

"I'm with the wife," William smirks.

"Theo? Joanna?"

I look down at my wife.

"I want to stay." She gets up from her position where she's sat beside Victoria and goes to stand in front of my father. He looks up at her and spits. Nicholas kicks him in his wounded leg, and he lets out a scream of pain.

"On your knees," Joanna commands, standing tall in front of him with her shoulders pulled back, and her head held high. He doesn't move, so she repeats her order, "On your knees."

Nicholas grabs him and pulls him up so that he bows low before her.

"If I could keep you here and subject you to what you did me, I would, but I don't think any of us want to keep you alive for that long. You don't deserve a moment more of our pain and worry. I will, however, thank you for one thing. For giving me Theo. My soul mate, and my savior. Despite who his father is, he's the kindest man I've ever met. I know we'll be gray and old, and in our bed together when we die. It will be peaceful and painless. Not like your death."

Tamara comes to Joanna's side and takes her hand.

"You stole my mother from me, and in a brutal way. She should be here to see the child I'm carrying welcomed into the world. You are a sick old man with twisted views on what is acceptable. In no way would your depraved thoughts about me ever be reciprocated. I'll enjoy your death. I hope you rot in hell." She pauses a moment. "But I also have to thank you. You didn't give me William. Well, I suppose you did in a way with your treatment of Victoria, but no, my thank you is for something else. You gave me an education, and one I'll use to ensure every trace of you is removed from the records. You'll be nothing. A nobody for eternity."

I help Victoria to her feet when she holds her hand out to me and assist her over to where the other two women are standing. With Tamara on one side of Joanna, Victoria stands on the other side of my wife and takes her hand.

"You stole my innocence from me, and my belief in a world that was better than the one I lived in. You destroyed my past so you could have a future. It's a shame you never realized how strong the daughter you raised actually is. I survived being given away like a possession to a wicked and ruthless society. I found my husband and my love, and as the Duchess of Oakfield, I'll bring peace for generations to come. That is what I thank you for. For being my father, in just the way you were. You created what you see in this room right now. Every action you've ever undertaken has led to this point. The point of your death and our triumph." My sister looks to me. "Do you want to say anything, Theo?"

I look at my father who has managed to spit out the tie that was stuffed in his mouth and is now starting to beg,

"Please, Theo, you can stop this with one word. I'll do whatever it takes. Don't be the monster these people have tried to turn you into."

I let out a laugh—it's a long barking one, and the entire room falls silent.

"You still believe after all of this you're innocent, don't you? That what you did was for the good of a future where women would be preyed on and abused." I pull my fist back and send it slamming into his face. My knuckles are still sore from my attack on Joanna's father and instantly smart. But I don't care when I see my father's nose break.

"Pull his shirt off," I order Nicholas who eyes me suspiciously. But when I unbuckle my belt, he realizes exactly what I mean to do. He strips my father of his crisp white shirt, which has been marred with a splattering of blood, and I take my belt and bring it crashing down on my father's back. He yells out and tries to shift, but William comes forward and holds him down. I repeat the process twenty times, harder and harder each time until his back is littered with cuts, oozing blood.

"Is that how you think a woman should be treated?" I ask my father, and he spits at my boot, so I kick him in the face. "Did you do that to Joanna?"

My wife comes to my side and places her hand on my shoulder.

"Yes," she tells me.

"Was there more?"

There are various sex toys littered around the room, which the men had planned to use on my sisters. I grab a large one and ram it down my father's throat.

"How about that?"

Joanna nods.

"Maybe I should go further? Make you truly understand what it's like to be a woman in your world."

William bends down and picks up a particularly large phallic shaped object.

"If you do, I say we use this one."

I shake my head.

"It's not something I particularly want to see, thank you. No, I think he gets the message. His actions have created a better man in me than he ever was, and that's why Joanna is now free. She's learned what happiness is, despite the demonic actions of a mad man who has half the balls I do."

"Phew." William wipes his brow. "I was worried. I've seen some sick things, but I'm getting too old for this shit. I'd rather just go home and fuck my wife senseless."

"William." Tamara whacks him on the shoulder.

"Sorry, can't help with the truth."

Nicholas coughs.

"Are we done?" he questions, and we all nod yes. "Who wants the honors?"

"Me." All three women say in unison. It's like a melody in my head. The three women left distraught at the hands of my father are ready to take back their power.

Joanna pulls her weapon back out while William hands Tamara his, and I give Victoria mine.

Nicholas positions my father on his knees and steps away from the path of any possible ricochets.

"Arthur Hamilton, former Viscount. I, Victoria Cavendish, Duchess of Oakfield and founding member of the new society of Oakfield find you guilty of offenses against our charter including the rape and murder of Elsie Bennett." Victoria points her weapon at our father.

"Arthur Hamilton, former Viscount. I, Tamara Cavendish, Countess of Lullington and founding member of the new society of Oakfield pass sentence of death upon you for offenses against our charter." Tamara follows suit.

Finally, Joanna steps up and points her weapon at my father.

"Arthur Hamilton, former Viscount. I, Joanna Hamilton, Countess of Linton and founding member of the new society of Oakfield strip you of your name and power by acting as your executioner."

Three guns fire and hit their target. My father slumps down to the ground—dead. Each woman places the gun down on the floor and walks over to their respective partner. Joanna nestles into my chest.

"Can we go home, now?"

I bring my lips to hers.

"Yes."

As we all leave the room, I turn around and take a final

look at the man who I worshipped for most of my life. It'll take a long while to absorb everything that has happened over the last few weeks, but with my loving wife at my side, I know that what she said about us growing gray and old together won't just be a dream. It'll be a reality, and a new Oakfield will emerge with me, Joanna, Nicholas, Victoria, William, and Tamara at the helm. A place of sanctuary, not violence. The past is dead. Long live the future.

EPILOGUE

ROSE WINDSOR, DUCHESS OF OAKFIELD

Thirty years later

"Hello and welcome to Oakfield hall. I want to thank you all for coming here today. My name is Rose Windsor and today I turned thirty years old and inherited my father's title and became Duchess of Oakfield. Thank you, daddy." I smile down at my father where he sits in the front row of the audience with his arm wrapped around my mother, he leans over and gives her a kiss and she kisses him back. I know that despite being sixty my father will take my mother back to their bedroom soon and I doubt they'll surface for the rest of the evening. It's a big embarrassment to me and my younger sister and two younger brothers how in love with each other they still are. Twins, Amelia and Jonathan, and little Reggie named after my father's childhood butler, all sit beside my parents. Amelia is engaged to be married to a man from New York and is only here for a few days before she returns to her fashion career in the states. She was recently asked to design the wedding dress of the actress Bethany Jolie when she married my dad's friend, Prince John. Jonathan runs the Oakfield estates for my father while Reggie is still at university studying finance and unsure what he wants to do with his future yet. Next to them sits my husband, Henry Windsor, we were married last year after being introduced at an art exhibition three years ago. I'm carrying our first child at the moment, but we've not told anyone yet as it's still early days. I know mum and dad will be thrilled when they find out. I'm ex cited to tell them. About ten years ago, mum sat me down and told me about how she and dad met. I've always known she had the Oakfield crest burnt into the skin on her thigh. I've never asked about it before, but it just felt like it was time. She told me how her father had given her to my dad as part of an old pact within the society. She'd been subjected to terrible trials by the previous Duke but her and my father had fallen in love and eventually managed to triumph over the man who would have been my grandad. It took me a long time to come to terms with what had happened. I'd packed my bags and travelled around the world for a few months as I allowed it all to sink in. It was the best thing I'd ever done though as it helped me when I eventually took over the new version of the Oakfield Society.

That is the other reason I stand in front of an audience on

my thirtieth birthday. It's because I'm handing out grants to a new intake of candidates to our scheme to help assist those who want to succeed in the world of art, drama and music.

I finish handing out the last certificate and step down from the plate. My cousin, Daphne stands their clapping her hands. She's the daughter of my Aunt Joanna and Uncle Theo. She's a few years younger than me and I've brought her into the society as my assistant because her knowledge of marketing matters is second to none. My aunt and uncle had difficultly conceiving her, I was told his was due to scaring, it wasn't until after my mother had told me the story of her meeting with my father than she told me how my aunt and uncle met. To have one grandfather who was a devil is unlucky but two, shameful. I can't believe what happened to Joanna and the fact it left her unable to conceive a child without IVF. Thankfully they had Daphne and then adopted three more children, Sebastian, Chloe and Frederick. You would never know that the last three aren't biological to them, they are loved just as much and told off when wrong in the same way. My uncle Theo can be a bit domineering and over protective especially of the girls, but my aunt Joanna seems to like it. She often calls him her saviour when I've been around. My uncle runs his estates which have been combined with the title of Linton which Joanna inherited from her father. Joanna spends a lot of her time doing photography and even has a gallery in London where she sells them from.

"You were so good." Daphne applauds me, "How are you feeling? Any sickness?" She hands me a flute full of water not champagne.

I roll my eyes at her. I can't keep a secret from my cousin. It's impossible.

"I'm good. Where is your mum and dad?" I laugh.

"Mum had a headache, they send their apologies. Dad was going to come but he said he better stay with mum in case she needed anything." Daphne doesn't need to say anything else, Uncle Theo and Aunt Joanna are just as amorous as my parents.

Henry comes to my side and brings me close to him kissing me passionately.

"I love it when you come over all boss lady. Maybe you could speak to me that way later." He winks and I run my tongue over my lips. I wish I could take him to bed now, I think I've inherited my parents passionate streak.

"I don't need to hear that about my niece." My uncle William coughs from behind us.

"Sorry Uncle William." I give him a welcoming kiss on the cheek.

"You did amazingly." My aunt Tamara joins him and congratulates me, "Your mother was feeling a little tired. Your father has taken her for a rest. They'll be back down to congratulate you later."

William lets out a loud snort.

"Not if he takes one of his Viagra tablets. He'll be fucking her all night."

Daphne and I both screw up our noses and stick out our tongues.

"Yuck! Uncle William."

"I know." He grabs a flute of champagne from a passing waiter. "One of those things I'm not supposed to talk about."

"Yes." Tamara whacks him on the shoulder and shakes her head.

"How about I say I'm going to wash some Viagra down with this champagne, so you better get that cute backside upstairs."

"You are just saying things to cross out the children now. Katherine and Oscar hate it when you do that." Aunt Joanna refers to my other cousins, their children. Katherine is an actress in Hollywood while Oscar still lives at Oakfield Hall. He is on the autism spectrum like my Uncle William, but I've never seen two parents so devoted to giving him love and reassurance over his diagnosis.

"Is it working." They both laugh together before disappearing and I know I won't see them again this evening. This party is now mine. A new generation is taking over. The sins of the past are dead, our futures are bright, and we have the power to make our own decisions. Everyone is happy. Everyone is free. That is what Oakfield is now, our sovereignty complete but no longer one of darkness because it is only filled with light and sex, lots of consensual sex.

THE END

I hope you've enjoyed the Dark Sovereignty Series. Look out for more Dark Romance from me soon.

Dark Sovereignty

Legacy of Succession, Book 1

Tainted Reasoning, Book 2
A Father's Insistence, Book 3

ACKNOWLEDGMENTS

First and always to my great friend, Charity Hendry, for always being there for me. For entertaining my crazy ideas and helping me bring them to fruition. Love you to bits.

To my editor, Tracy Roelle, and proofreader, Sheena Taylor, you polish my books so that they shine brightly. I'm lucky to have such a good team.

To my street team, thank you so much for all you that you do to get my books out in the reader world.

To Yvonne, for not only beta reading and offering me advice but for organizing so much when it comes to conventions. I'd be lost without you.

To my family, thank you for all the support that you give me.

Finally, to all the readers who have embraced me as an author.

I'm so glad that you enjoy the stories my mind creates. I hope I'm able to give you many more years of pleasure.

THE CONTROL SERIES

The Control Series: A dramatic, witty, and sensual suspense romance set predominantly in London.

Surrendered Control, The Control Series, Book 1:

Divided Control, The Control Series, Book 2:

Misguided Control, The Control Series, Book 3:

Controlling Darkness, The Control Series, Book 4:

Controlling Heritage, The Control Series, Book 5:

Controlling Disgrace, The Control Series, Book 6:

Controlling the Past, The Control Series, Book 7:

THE GLACIAL BLOOD

The Touch of Snow, The Glacial Blood Series, Book 1

Fighting the Lies, The Glacial Blood Series, Book 2:

Fallen for Shame, The Glacial Blood Series, Book 3:

Shattered Fears, The Glacial Blood Series, Book 4:

Coming Soon to the Glacial Blood Series...
Hidden Pain – Hunter, Lily and Kingsley's story
Stolen Choices – Katia's story
Power of a Myth – Molly and Hayden's story
A Deadly Affair – Jessica's story
Banishing Regrets – Kas' story

BECAUSE HE'S PERFECT ANTHOLOGY

Because He's Perfect is a charity anthology with all proceeds being donated to the Movember Foundation. Twenty-four authors ranging from first time writers to long-term storytellers, seek to dispel all the myths from the romance world about what a perfect hero should be.

Emotional or physical disabilities and illnesses are nothing to be ashamed of; in fact they can make a man. With the inclusion of a poignantly emotional foreword by NYT best-selling author, Carrie Ann Ryan, this anthology will take you on a journey through comedic laughs, sweet contemporary romance, and into the world of darkness and bizarre.

Joining the authors on their quest are one graphic artist, one photographer, and two models donating their time and efforts to this project, which has inspired all involved.

We hope you will enjoy what you read, 'Because He's Perfect'.

ONLY $0.99 to Pre-order.

Amazon:

Goodreads:

BookBub:

Foreword - Carrie Ann Ryan

Authors:

Abigail Davies

Alice La Roux

Ally Vance

Anna Blakely

Anna Edwards

Ashleigh Giannoccaro

Claire Marta

Danielle Dickson

Elle Boon

Jo-Anne Joseph

KA Sands

Lexi C Foss

Lexxie Couper

Maria Macdonald

Morgan Campbell

Murphy Wallace

Renee Harless

Samantha Lewis

Sienna Grant

Tracie Delaney

Victoria L. James

Yolanda Olson

Models

Sean Brady

Christopher John

Photographers

Christopher John at CJC Photography

David Wills

Graphic Artist

Charity Hendry at Judged by the Cover.

ABOUT THE AUTHOR

I am a British author, from the depths of the rural countryside near London. In a previous life, I was an accountant from the age of twenty-one. I still do that on occasions, but most of my life is now spent intermingling writing while looking after my husband, two children and two cats (probably in the inverse order to the one listed!). When I have some spare time, I can also be found writing poetry, baking cakes (and eating them), or behind a camera snapping like a mad paparazzi.

I'm an avid reader who turned to writing to combat my depression and anxiety. I have a love of traveling and like to bring this to my stories to give them the air of reality.

I like my heroes hot and hunky with a dirty mouth, my heroines demure but with spunk, and my books full of dramatic suspense.

CONNECT WITH ANNA EDWARDS
www.AuthorAnnaEdwards.com
Newsletter: http://eepurl.com/cwxJ6v
Email: anna1000edwards@gmail.com

MEET THE AUTHOR

I'll be at the following signings:

21-24 February - Wild Wicked Weekend, San Antonio, Texas, USA
2nd March – Leeds Author Event, Leeds, UK
1st June – Heart of Steel, Sheffield, UK.
18-19 October – Shameless, Orlando, Florida, US

40526029R00134

Printed in Poland
by Amazon Fulfillment
Poland Sp. z o.o., Wrocław